THEY THOUGHT
JOHN BONNIWELL
WAS DEAD . . .

Bullets slammed through the thin walls of the stagecoach office as the frightened passengers huddled together.

"Stay away from the windows," the man they knew as John Wells told them. Then he stepped outside.

He faced Jim Malachy and his drunken, rioting mob quietly, his hands hanging loosely at his sides. "Drop the guns, Malachy," he said "Tell your men to drop theirs."

Somewhere in the crowd a voice rang out, shrill with fear. "It's Bonniwell! John Bonniwell. He's alive!"

Frank Gruber's
PEACE MARSHAL

Bantam Books by Frank Gruber

FORT STARVATION
PEACE MARSHAL

Peace Marshal
Frank Gruber

PEACE MARSHAL
A Bantam Book / March 1958
2nd printing ...... September 1963
3rd printing .... July 1972
4th printing .... April 1981

All rights reserved.
Copyright 1939 by Frank Gruber.
Copyright renewed 1966 by Frank Gruber.
This book may not be reproduced in whole or in part, by mimeograph or any other means, without permission.
For information address: Bantam Books, Inc.

ISBN 0-553-14539-8

Published simultaneously in the United States and Canada

Bantam Books are published by Bantam Books, Inc. Its trademark, consisting of the words "Bantam Books" and the portrayal of a bantam, is Registered in U.S. Patent and Trademark Office and in other countries. Marca Registrada. Bantam Books, Inc., 666 Fifth Avenue, New York, New York 10103.

PRINTED IN THE UNITED STATES OF AMERICA

13 12 11 10 9 8 7 6 5 4

Contents

I	THE TWO BROTHERS	1
II	THE LAW OF THE COLT	8
III	TRAIL TOWN	21
IV	LEAD FOR HIRE	32
V	AMBUSH	39
VI	LAW MAN	46
VII	BOOM TOWN	61
VIII	UNSEEN FOES	72
IX	SIX-GUN LAW	86
X	"GIVE ME YOUR GUNS!"	96
XI	FRAMED	113
XII	FINISH FIGHT	125
XIII	SHOWDOWN	137

Chapter One

THE TWO BROTHERS

THE HANSOM CAB turned down the tree-shaded street opposite Gramercy Park and the silk-hatted driver scanned the numbers of the houses as his sleek horse trotted along. Finally he saw the number he was seeking and pulled up the horse. It stopped before the most imposing brownstone house in the block.

The cabby climbed down from his perch and said to the solitary passenger, "Here it is, Mister."

A lean man in a Prince Albert climbed out. He drew a half dollar from the pocket of his silk waistcoat. Then he looked at the brownstone house and a pleased look crossed his face. He put the half dollar back in his pocket and fished out a silver dollar instead. He handed it to the cabby and said, magnanimously, "Keep the change, driver."

He turned back to the brownstone house and smacked his lips.

"I'm glad I played my hunch," he said to himself. "Ferd seems to have done very well for himself."

He crossed the sidewalk, climbed three stairs and lifted a brass door knocker. He banged it against the metal plate.

Presently a liveried butler opened the door. The smile of the lean man widened. "Tell Mr. Ferdinand Barat that his brother is calling."

The butler bowed. "Very good, sir. Will you come in, sir?"

Jeff Barat followed the butler into a large room. The butler disappeared through a doorway and Jeff Barat appraised the rich furnishings of the room. "Not *bad*," he said aloud. He tugged gently at his coat lapels and pulled out his starched cuffs.

He heard a heavy step and turned to face his brother.

"Ferd!"

The man who came into the room was about forty-five, seven or eight years older than Jeff Barat. He was a rather heavy man and wore a tailored Prince Albert, dark striped trousers and a flowered waistcoat.

"Jeff!" he said. "After all these years!"

They shook hands warmly, then stepped back to survey one another. Jeff Barat grinned slyly. "You've gotten fat, Ferd. You look like a rich man."

The older brother seemed to wince a little. "You don't look a year older yourself. What is it now—nine years since you..."

Jeff Barat chuckled. "Since I skipped Mr. Lincoln's draft? Yes, it's just about nine years. It *was* in '63, wasn't it?"

"Yes. It caused me considerable embarrassment at the time. You know I would have given you the three hundred to pay the substitute."

"It wasn't the money—it was the principle of the thing. And that whippersnapper of a lieutenant—I never took that from any man."

"I gave his family some money," said Fred Barat, hastily. He took a deep breath. "Where've you been during these years, Jeff? You never wrote a line, you know."

"I was in California for a year or two; then I took a trip to Idaho." A reminiscent grin played about Jeff Barat's mouth. "I was at the Alder Gulch diggings for awhile. Struck it rich——"

"Why, that's fine, Jeff!" exclaimed his brother.

Jeff chuckled. "I sold out for twenty-two thousand and ran it up to fifty thousand at faro. And then—I lost it all in a single night."

Ferdinand Barat's face fell. "All?"

"Every dollar. In Cheyenne, Wyoming, when they were building the railroad, I borrowed ten dollars and a pack of cards and ran it up to one hundred and ten thousand." Jeff rubbed his chin with the back of his hand. "I lost it all in Utah!"

Ferdinand Barat drew a thin cigar from his pocket and bit off the end. He did not offer one to his brother. "And today —how are you fixed today?"

Jeff looked around the room and picked out the best chair. He sat down in it, stretched out his long legs and grinned at his brother. "Today, Ferd, I'm flat broke. And if you think I'm going to make a touch, you're quite right."

For a moment the older man scowled. Then he sighed heavily. "After all, you *are* my brother."

Jeff sighed, too. He'd wondered if he'd lost the touch during the years. Evidently he hadn't. He said: "Ferd, I read a piece about you in a St. Louis paper. You've been in railroads with Mr. Vanderbilt and Mr. Fisk and some of the boys."

"A month ago," said Ferdinand Barat, "I was worth ten million dollars. I had them licked—and then they ganged up on me."

Jeff studied his brother's face. "But they didn't get all of it?"

"Just about. I may have a quarter million or so, but that's all."

Jeff Barat got up quickly from his chair.

"A quarter million!" he cried. "That's plenty. I've got a proposition in Kansas that'll make your Wall Street stuff look like small potatoes——"

"I wouldn't give you a quarter million dollars for all of Kansas!" exclaimed Ferdinand Barat.

"Ah, but that's where you're wrong, Ferd. All you Easterners are wrong about Kansas. You think of it as a heap of sand with a herd of buffalo and a few coyotes. And you're wrong, Ferd, dead wrong. They're building railroads in Kansas. You know railroads, Ferd."

"As far as I'm concerned," retorted the older brother, "there are no more railroads."

Jeff Barat brushed the remark aside. "Hear me through, Ferd. Down in Texas there are millions and millions of cattle. They let them run wild during the war and the country's overrun with them. They're worthless—in Texas. Some of the ranchers kill them for the hide and tallow, for which they get from two to three dollars. And here in the East, you're crying for beef. A Texas steer is worth thirty-five to forty dollars in New York. It'll bring thirty in Chicago, twenty to twenty-five in Kansas, at railhead."

"True, perhaps," conceded Ferdinand. "But how are you going to get your steer from Texas to Kansas?"

"Like they've been doing it since 1867—overland, up the Chisholm Trail. They drove thirty-five thousand head up that trail in 1867. Last year two million Texas steers reached Kansas."

"Two million?" exclaimed Ferdinand, incredulous.

"Two million. And buyers in Kansas fought to get them."

Ferdinand's eyes became thoughtful. "I can check that, Jeff. Go ahead. What is this million dollar proposition you mentioned a minute ago? How do *we* come in on that?"

Jeff's nostrils flared in triumph. He brought two folded maps from his pocket.

"This is a map of the United States—west of the Mississippi. You know all about railroad stocks, Ferd. But do you know anything about the railroads themselves? This line here is the Union Pacific Railroad, which was joined with the Central Pacific in Utah, less than three years ago. Here, notice where it runs through Nebraska, Wyoming? Its closest point to Texas is in northern Colorado. Now——" Jeff put the first map aside and unfolded the other.

"This is a large scale map of Kansas, the Indian Nations and Texas. Up here is the Kansas Pacific Railroad. Here is Abilene, which from 1867 to 1871 received nine-tenths of all the Texas cattle. It was, last year, the busiest, ripsnortingest little town in all Kansas. This year grass is growing on its streets. The cattle trade went to Caldwell, Newton and Hays City."

Jeff paused a moment and looked at his brother. "Study this map closely. Notice the position of the Kansas Pacific Railroad, the location of these towns that are today getting the cattle trade. Here is the Chisholm Trail, over which every head of cattle comes to Kansas. Suppose the railroad went right down here into the southwest corner of Kansas? Suppose a shipping point was located at this point?"

"Why, I imagine it would get most of the cattle trade. It's a hundred miles closer to the origin of the cattle herds."

"Right!" cried Jeff Barat. "And that's where we come in. A railroad *is* going to this spot. A town *is* going to be laid out there—and no one knows it yet but you and I."

"Do *we* build it?"

"No, it's already being built. In two months it will reach this spot on the Chisholm Trail, where there's now a store and a half dozen mud-covered shacks. They call it Broken Lance. The minute the railroad comes to it, Broken Lance will become a city, bigger than Abilene. It'll be the greatest boom town the West ever saw. A million head of cattle will come to it even this first year. And you and I will collect a toll of two, three, or four dollars on every steer that reaches Broken Lance. Why? Because we will own every acre of land in twenty miles. Because the drovers can't take their steers across our private property without paying us."

"Go on," said Ferdinand.

"We do that for a year, perhaps two. Then the railroad will be built down into Texas. What happens to us then?

"We're still in Kansas. We're the biggest ranchers in the country. Why? Because we took our toll from the drovers in cattle, instead of money. We own a hundred thousand cattle, which cost us nothing. We're nine hundred miles closer to the market and we can undersell any Texas rancher."

Ferdinand Barat shook his head.

"Perhaps we can acquire the land around this railroad point. The rest of your scheme, though, is predicated upon your being able to exact a toll from the Texas drovers. Ah—suppose they refuse to pay? I've heard they're very harsh men down in that country. Every man, they tell me, carries a gun."

"Ferd——"

"Yes?"

Jeff Barat looked thoughtfully at his brother. Then suddenly he shook his right arm. Ferd Barat blinked. A double-barreled derringer had appeared miraculously in his brother's hand.

"Ferd," said Jeff, slowly, "will I shock you when I say I've been making my living as a gambler these last dozen years?"

"A lot of men gamble," said Ferd Barat. "I like a good game myself."

Jeff nodded. "It so happens I have a peculiar ability aside from gambling. I am a rather famous personage out West. I'm known as one of the fastest gun throwers in four states."

Ferd Barat's eyes widened. "You—you've killed someone?"

Jeff Barat did not blink an eyelash. "More than a dozen men have drawn against me, Ferd. I'm alive. In the matter I outlined to you, my reputation will be an invaluable asset. What's more, I know a couple of men—friends of mine—who'll string along with me. What we can't get by money we'll take by force."

Ferd Barat looked for a long moment at his lean brother. Then he sighed. "I wish, Jeff, you'd been here last month. You might have been some assistance to me."

"It's a deal, then?"

"I don't know. Perhaps. Naturally, I want to go into it some more. I want to verify some of the things you've told me. In the meantime, stay here with me."

Jeff Barat smacked his lips. "In that case, I'll go down to the Astor House and get my things. I wasn't just sure how you'd react to the return of the prodigal, and so I checked in there. I don't mind spending a couple of weeks in the old town. It'll be fun!"

Jeff's ideas of fun did not coincide with those of his older brother, but Ferdinand did not comment on the matter until the third day, when Jeff, ready for the evening's entertainment, said:

"I say, Ferd, how about some change?"

"Change?" asked Ferdinand. "I gave you five hundred the day before yesterday."

"Yes, of course," chuckled Jeff. "But that was the day before yesterday."

The older man rubbed his chin. After a moment, he said, "All right. If you do everything on such a scale I guess we'll *have* to make money on that cattle deal."

"You're all set, then?"

Ferdinand nodded. "Just about. I verified the railroad survey today. Tonight I'm seeing a man who's been out in that country. You see, I want to get a picture of things out there from a disinterested person. By the way, why don't you come with me? I think you'd be interested in meeting this man."

"What's his name?"

"Judson. He's a writer."

"I never heard of him. I did have an engagement with a young lady I met last night, but if the deal's about set, I might as well drop her now as in a few days."

Ferdinand took his brother to a club on Fifth Avenue. Jeff had never seen so many white waistcoats at one time in his life.

Ferdinand's friend was waiting for them.

"My brother Jeff," Ferdinand said to the writer. "He's just returned from an extensive residence in the West."

Judson held out his hand.

"Jeff Barat," he said musingly. "That name has a familiar ring to it. And your face—I'm almost sure I've seen it somewhere."

"Perhaps you have," said Jeff Barat. "But I don't remember meeting anyone by the name of Judson before."

"Oh, but that isn't the name by which they know me out West. Out there I use the name of Buntline—Ned Buntline!"

Jeff Barat's lips seemed to tighten. "Ned Buntline! You're the man that writes that stuff about Buffalo Bill. The bang-bang kid stuff."

Buntline smiled, but there wasn't much warmth in it.

"Perhaps my books do appeal to many boys," he said, "but my publishers tell me quite a few grownups read them, too."

"That's true," said Ferdinand Barat. "I don't happen to have read one myself, but I've been told Mr. Buntline's books have an enormous circulation. And you have a wide acquaintance among Western men, haven't you, Mr. Buntline?"

"Yes, I have. I know Mr. Cody intimately. And Masterson and Hickok and quite a few others. I've traveled extensively through the West, gathering material for my books. Most of my characters are patterned after real personages, you know. The incidents are based on things that actually took place."

"Like Wild Bill Hickok killing eleven of the McKanlas gang at one time?" Jeff Barat asked sarcastically.

"Mr. Hickok hasn't affirmed that," said Buntline. "Nor has he denied it. The thing may sound fantastic perhaps to the people who don't really know the West. Mr. Hickok's exploit is eleven years old. But I know of one that almost equaled it which happened only a few months ago. And I'm in a position to speak of it with authenticity. I didn't see the fight, but I was in Haleyville when it happened. I saw the bodies within ten minutes after the fight. There were *four*. All were killed by one man, the marshal of Haleyville."

"You mean John Bonniwell?"

"Yes. The four men he killed were notorious gunfighters. They'd sought him out to kill him. Instead they were killed themselves."

"And so was Bonniwell."

"No, I understand he was badly wounded, but he was taken to a hospital in Kansas City."

"Just talk. The sheriff buried him. He was in a tight spot and he spread the rumor that Bonniwell was only wounded, figuring it'd keep the Texas men quiet for a spell. Bonniwell did have the Indian sign on them."

"You're familiar with Kansas matters, Mr. Barat," said Ned Buntline thoughtfully. "I wonder—no, I don't think so. Knowing your brother——"

"What? If I'm Jeff Barat, the gambler?" Jeff Barat grinned thinly.

"Are you?"

"Yes."

The expression on Ned Buntline's face was comical to

see. Jeff Barat laughed out loud. "You didn't expect to ever meet Jeff Barat in a club on Fifth Avenue in New York, did you, Mr. Buntline?"

"Hardly," said the writer.

Ferd Barat tried to smooth over the difficult situation, but Ned Buntline made an excuse and withdrew after a moment or two.

The older Barat shook his head. "All right, Jeff. We're starting tomorrow. Judson's reaction toward you is enough for me. I wanted to be sure about you. You've enough of me in you, Jeff, to succeed. We'll go out there. In two or three years I'll come back here and teach Vanderbilt and the others a few new tricks. At the moment they've got too much money for me. But they'll hear from me again."

Chapter Two

LAW OF THE COLT

JOHN BONNIWELL was walking. Of course the male nurse lent a steadying hand. But it was good to use his legs. There had been a time when he hadn't been sure if he'd ever use them again.

They made two slow, complete circuits of the broad veranda. It was spring and the sun was warm, life-giving. Bonniwell inhaled great drafts of sweet Missouri air.

"There you are, Mr. Wells," said the nurse as he brought Bonniwell back to his wheel chair. "Sit here now and soak up some of that good sun for an hour or so. It'll make a new man of you."

Bonniwell would have thanked the man, but he was annoyed. During his walk someone had brought out another invalid and seated her in a chair only five or six feet from Bonniwell's own.

He didn't look directly at her. Not right away. He'd caught a quick glance of her as the nurse seated him, but when the man left he looked steadily out over the cheap, unpainted board houses and muddy street that was St. Louis in 1872.

He thought: "She's watching me now. In a little while she's going to talk, tell me how glorious the sun is."

She said: "Isn't spring wonderful?"

He waited a cold moment, then turned brooding eyes on her. He couldn't see much of her because she was wrapped to the chin in a heavy, woolly robe. He could see her face. It was a bit thin and the smooth skin was whiter than Bonniwell liked to see in anyone. Her eyes were enormous, her hair golden blond. The sun shining on it made it look like fine silk.

She was young. She looked to be not more than eighteen or nineteen, but was probably two or three years older than that. By city standards she was beautiful. Farther West folks would have thought her too frail and delicate.

"Spring's always good," he admitted grudgingly.

"You've been here a long time?"

"Yes."

She smiled brightly. "You're from the West, aren't you?"

He nodded.

She knew that the conversation was one-sided, yet she persisted. "That's why I spoke to you. You see, I'm being discharged next week. Then I'm going West to—to pick up some weight. My uncle has a ranch in Kansas. I'm going to visit him. He lives near Broken Lance. Do you know where that is?"

He looked at her through narrowed lids. "Broken Lance? Your folks sending you there?"

"Yes. Uncle didn't seem to want me to come. He said it was a bit wild out there, but Dad—well, he hasn't enough money to send me anywhere else. And the doctors say I must live outdoors a while. In a drier climate. So it's Broken Lance, Kansas."

Her uncle had been right. Broken Lance *was* wild. It was in the heart of the Indian and buffalo country. It wasn't a woman's country, unless the woman could drive a span of oxen and shoot a rifle.

This girl wasn't the sort. She wouldn't thrive in Broken Lance, despite the dry, healthy climate that was supposed to be good for sick lungs.

"You didn't answer," the girl's voice cut into Bonniwell's thoughts. "Do you know where Broken Lance is?"

He bit his lip and nodded. "I've been through it."

"You have?" she exclaimed eagerly. "Then tell me about it. Is it like Uncle Ollie said?"

"Did he say Broken Lance wasn't a town? That there're only a few houses there?"

"Oh yes, he tried to discourage me from coming." She smiled. "I'm being forced on him. But tell me—have you ever met my uncle? Or heard of him?"

"I don't know. I don't know his name."

"Oh, how stupid of me! My name's Eleanor Simmons. My uncle's Oliver Simmons."

He whistled softly. She was Ollie Simmons' niece. He wouldn't have guessed it in a thousand guesses. He acknowledged her introduction. "My name's—John Wells." That was the name he had been using at the hospital.

"How do you do, Mr. Wells," she said. "I—you seemed to know my uncle. What sort of a man is he?"

"Don't you know?"

"I've never seen him. He went west before the war. Is he tall or short? Genial or a—a crosspatch?"

He grinned faintly. "Your uncle is one of the leading citizens out there. No one has ever said a word against him. Not in his hearing," he added under his breath. Ollie Simmons was a lobo wolf among coyotes.

Bonniwell ran a hand across his lean face; a face that was ordinarily sun-tanned and weather-beaten, but now pallid from his long siege in the hospital.

Eleanor Simmons saw his apparent movement of weariness and was all sympathy. "I shouldn't question you like this. You're very ill, they told me."

"Did they tell you from what?" he asked quickly.

She shook her head. "No, they said you'd been hurt in an accident."

Five bullets in him. Yes, it had been an "accident." He said, "I'm not sick any more. Just a bit weak. I'll be leaving here in a couple of weeks."

"And you're going back west? To Broken Lance?"

"Oh, I didn't come from Broken Lance. Haleyville was my headquarters."

"Haleyville? I seem to recall the name. It's noted for something or other, isn't it?"

He waited just a moment before he said: "It's trail's end. On the railroad. That's probably why you've heard of it."

"Perhaps. What is it, nurse?"

A buxom woman had approached her chair. "Time for you to go in, Miss Simmons. It's getting a bit chilly."

"I hadn't noticed. Well, all right." She smiled brightly at Bonniwell as the nurse turned her chair and wheeled it into the hospital.

Bonniwell sighed after she had gone. If her uncle didn't think she ought to come to Broken Lance and her father didn't have the money, why didn't Ollie Simmons loan it to them and have the girl go to southern California? The climate was dry and warm there. Eleanor Simmons had no business in Broken Lance, Kansas.

He made three complete circuits of the veranda the next day. He didn't lean once on the arm of the nurse. He wasn't even tired when he sat down in the chair by the railing. The weather was crisper today. Probably too cool.

No, it wasn't. She came out five minutes later.

"Hello, Mr. Wells," she greeted him cheerily. "I was hoping you'd be out here. I want to hear some more about Kansas. There's a woman in my ward from Kansas—Wichita. I asked her about Broken Lance. She'd never heard of it. But she knew about your home, Haleyville. What she said made me recall what I'd heard about it. It was that awful riot they had there last fall. It was in all the papers. It was the time the sheriff or marshal, or whatever they call him, killed all those—what were they, rustlers?"

They hadn't been exactly rustlers, Taylor and Smiley and the others. A decent rustler wouldn't have slept in the same bed with them. They had, however, been good pistol men. They'd put five bullets into Bonniwell before he had finally downed them.

He hadn't known, though, that the Eastern newspapers had printed anything about it. Out in Kansas they considered such stuff "local news."

He passed up her direct lead about Haleyville, shifted the conversation to the better things of Kansas. He told her of the rich country out there, the sandy loam the earlier settlers had passed up as too bare for good crops. Yet it was the finest wheatland in the country, when the soil was plowed deep.

Some of the settlers had hundreds of acres in wheat now, and found it more profitable than cattle. In a few years the railroad would reach all the way down to Texas, and then the Chisholm Trail would be plowed over, the trail towns forgotten. Haleyville and Broken Lance, and Dodge and

Abilene would become sleepy country towns, safe even for girls like Eleanor Simmons.

She told him about herself. Her father was a doctor over in Benton. It was only a small village and the citizens were unusually healthy. It had strained her father's resources to send her here to the hospital in St. Louis.

She pulled John Bonniwell out of his natural reticence. He talked with her every day a half hour or more. He told her about the plains country, the far West. He had been to California twice, to Oregon and the Black Hills. He told her nothing about *himself*.

He'd hunted buffalo, hauled freight. She asked him questions. She ran down every little detail of whatever the topic happened to be. When he wasn't with her he manufactured things to tell her, long stories that would prevent her from asking personal questions. He spent two days describing placer mining in California; one entire period he talked about a snow-storm in Montana. And four afternoons about the Union Pacific Railroad.

And then it was the day she was to leave the hospital. A phaeton was out front to take her to the depot on Poplar Street. Bonniwell was on the veranda when she came out. She wore a dress that fitted tightly at her waist and billowed out into a wide skirt. And a bustle. She had on a green hat with a bit of fur trimming and a silk ribbon tied under her chin. There was a touch of color in her cheeks now.

Bonniwell looked at her and felt bleak inside. She was going away, out of his life.

She was sober.

"Will I meet you out there, John?" she asked. "Out there in Kansas?"

He wanted to tell her, yes, he'd see her in Kansas—in Broken Lance. He wanted to tell her that and he wanted to go to Broken Lance himself. But he couldn't do either. Because he was John Bonniwell and she didn't know it.

He said; "I don't know if I'll get to Kansas. I'm thinking of going to Texas."

"But you said the Chisholm Trail runs into Texas, and that goes straight through Broken Lance."

"Yes, it does," he admitted. "But I'm going to east Texas. My old captain wrote me not so long ago that there were chances for a man in East Texas."

"Your captain? You didn't tell me you were in the army." She realized suddenly that despite the daily talks she'd had with this lean, sober man during the past weeks, she really knew very little about him. He'd never even mentioned being in the war, and it is the commonest thing in the world for a man to say, "When I was in the army. . . ."

"Yes," he replied, "I was in the army. Three years."

"The North?"

He nodded. "Third Illinois Infantry. I——" He grinned faintly—"I even got to be a corporal."

Her forehead crinkled. "I'd have thought you too young for the war."

"I really was. When I enlisted in '62 I was sixteen."

She did a bit of quick mental arithmetic. "That makes you twenty-six now."

Only twenty-six? It seemed as though he had been around much longer than that. The three years of the war had seemed thirty. And the years since—why, he'd been out in the West a hundred years! It seemed that long.

A coachman came out with two carpetbags.

"Ready, Miss Simmons?" he said.

She held out her hand.

"Good-by," she said. "If you *should* come to Broken Lance——"

He smiled and said, "Good-by." And then she was walking down the short flight of stairs, climbing into the carriage. She looked back at him and waved and he said to himself, "This should have happened eight years ago."

The hospital days were long then. But at last the doctor tapped his chest, prodded here and there and said, "You're a well man, Mr. Wells. Which is something I never expected to say to you last fall, when I dug all that lead out of you."

He didn't really want to go to Texas. He was a Northerner, and down there in Texas they were still fighting the war. Bonniwell had met Texans in Kansas. They had put five bullets in him. A hundred Texas men with money in their pockets and liquor in their stomachs would consider the conflict between Bonniwell and the men of Texas a blood feud and be gunning for him.

But what could he do? After paying the hospital bills he had only three hundred dollars. St. Louis was not for him. He was an outdoor man.

In the far West, thousands of men were grubbing and washing for specks of yellow metal. On the plains the hunters were slaughtering the great buffalo herds.

Bonniwell had scraped and washed for gold; he had killed too many buffalo. The zest for those things was gone. Captain Skinner had written him to come to Texas, but Bonniwell wasn't enthusiastic about that. There was one alternative. Somewhere out in Kansas or Colorado Tom Waggoner was building a railroad. Tom was the best friend he had in the world. He could no doubt find some sort of job for Bonniwell. It was a little too close to his old stamping grounds, but mixing with a different class of people he might lose his identity.

He stayed a day at the Planters Hotel in St. Louis. Then he packed his carpetbag and went to the railroad station. The next day he was in Kansas City.

Bonniwell walked past the police station and one or two men looked at his lean face and did not greet him. His illness had changed his appearance. His months in the hospital had made his skin several shades lighter.

He bought a railroad ticket to Baker, Kansas.

The train was crowded. There were women on it. Women of the effete East, other women not so effete, in fancy satins and silks, with carmined lips and rouged cheeks.

There were men on the train in silk hats and frock coats. Some of them were business men, some—usually those with the most expensive silk hats and the finest broadcloth coats with velvet collars—buffalo hunters, who had squandered a month's earnings on finery in which to disport for a few weeks; men who had sold their season's work and headed for St. Louis or farther east for brief vacations and were now returning to the plains, where they would pawn, gamble away or discard their fancy clothes and outfit themselves again with the buckskin of their callings.

Two or three poker games were going on. The conductor made some feeble protest about "gambling on trains" as the train pulled out of Kansas City, but he was ignored completely.

Bonniwell remained seated by the window the first two hours out of Kansas City. Then, the monotony of the scenery palling on him, he got up and walked back to the rear of the coach, to watch a poker game. He looked on for only a minute before he realized that this game was a bit more than ordinary. There were four men in the game, three of them wearing silk hats. The fourth man wore buckskin, but he had a huge stack of bills and gold coins before him. His clothing did not mean poverty.

The man who was dealing at the moment was about thirty-seven, perhaps a year or two younger. His fingers were long and supple and he dealt the cards with swift, sure movements. He was a lean man, lean almost to the point of being consumptive. His mouth was twisted into a sardonic smile. Directly across from him sat a man who seemed to be his older brother. A man of forty-five, but without the lean man's pallid complexion; a ruddy man with a long, carefully trimmed mustache, well manicured nails. His hands were clumsier than the younger dealer's.

The fourth man was a middle-aged cattleman, even if he did wear a silk hat.

The shabby man opened the pot for ten dollars and was promptly raised twenty. When the lean dealer swept in the pot a couple of minutes later, there was over a hundred dollars in it. Bonniwell caught the man's eyes.

The man smiled. "Want to sit in?"

Bonniwell nodded. "Looks like an interesting game." They made room for him and he sat down. "My name's Barat," said the lean man. "Jeff Barat. This is my brother, Ferdinand Barat."

The others introduced themselves. The man in buckskin said his name was Woeltjen. The rancher called himself Pearson. Bonniwell gave the name he had used for the past few months—John Wells.

He brought out a hundred dollars and put it on the table before him.

"Is this enough to start?" he asked.

"Yes, if you've more behind it," said Jeff Barat. He passed the cards to his older brother, who began to shuffle clumsily.

Jeff Barat studied Bonniwell's face. "Haven't I seen you somewhere?"

Bonniwell shrugged. "I've been in St. Louis since last fall. Have you been there?"

"Only passing through."

The buffalo hunter, Woeltjen, opened the pot for ten dollars. Bonniwell, with a pair of tens, stayed. Pearson raised twenty dollars and was promptly raised the same amount by Jeff Barat. Ferdinand Barat gave careful consideration to his cards, then called. The others were satisfied.

Woeltjen drew three cards. Bonniwell, on a hunch, held a queen with his tens and drew two. Pearson took only one card. Jeff Barat showed even white teeth in a smile and drew three cards.

Bonniwell drew another ten and an ace. He riffled the cards together and laid them flat on the table, face down. Woeltjen made a big show of counting out forty dollars. "Poker's goin' up, folks," he announced.

Bonniwell picked up his cards, looked at them and laid them down again. Then he looked sharply at Jeff Barat, began counting out money and looked again at Barat. He threw forty dollars into the pot.

Pearson tossed his cards into the discard. He had raised before the draw on a possible flush. Barat smiled thinly, counted out forty dollars and added more to it. He shoved it all into the center of the table.

"And one hundred," he said pleasantly.

Woeltjen growled deep in his throat, scowled furiously and after two or three false moves to count out money, tossed in his cards. The older Barat also dropped out.

Bonniwell got out all the money he had in his pockets. "And forty. I'd just as soon drop out after one hand as a dozen."

Jeff Barat's face showed no emotion at all. He counted out the forty and said, "I have a pair of kings."

Woeltjen howled. "And I threw away three eights!"

"They wouldn't have been good," said Bonniwell. "I have three tens." He laid them down and began pulling in the pot.

"You don't bluff," said Jeff Barat.

Bonniwell made a deprecating gesture. Barat had merely tested Bonniwell. He was a ferocious poker player, absolutely without mercy, but he seldom bluffed. Bonniwell found that out several pots later.

The buffalo hunter lost steadily, hundreds of dollars. Pearson played a close game and lost a little. Ferdinand Barat played clumsily but his brother spared him, and his losses, while heavy, were not as big as the buffalo hunter's. Bonniwell played his usual game, entirely without emotion, as the cards came. He won. Not as much as Jeff Barat, but enough. At the end of an hour he was ahead over a thousand dollars.

The train stopped at a station for ten minutes, then rolled on again. The buffalo hunter's gold was gone and a good many of his bills. He swore roundly but without rancor every time he lost a pot.

The train stopped. Bonniwell, his mind on his cards, thought nothing of it until Jeff Barat's moderate voice seemed suddenly loud. He realized it was because of the hush that had fallen upon the car. He looked up—and saw the two masked men at the far end of the car.

One of them spoke. "All right, just sit tight and no one'll be hurt!"

A woman screamed. One of the masked men marched down the aisle. There was a Colt in either hand.

"A holdup!" yelped Woeltjen. He started reaching for the gun at his thigh underneath the table, but Barat stopped him with a word. "Don't!"

The masked man stopped in the aisle, five feet away.

"That's a lot of money you boys got there!" he said in a calm voice.

"It is," said Jeff Barat.

The bandit made a swift movement. The gun in his left hand slid into his holster and a small gunny sack that had been tucked under his belt flipped to the table. "Put it in there—all of it."

Jeff Barat made no move. His older brother, his face white and tense, snarled, "Fine country you brought me to, Jeff!"

Bonniwell was looking steadily at the masked man's eyes. They were cold and pale blue through the slits in the cloth mask. The man finally sensed that Bonniwell was staring at him and his eyes met Bonniwell's.

"*You* put the money in the sack," he said.

Bonniwell picked up the sack, tossed his own money into it and then quickly gathered together the rest. He knew that his card companions were staring hostilely at him. When all the money on the table was in the bag, he shoved it to the edge of the table. The bandit did not pick it up.

"No," he said, "I think Mr. Barat has more money."

Jeff Barat scowled. "A few dollars. You want that, too?"

"Not yours," replied the bandit. "Your brother's."

Ferdinand Barat gasped. "Me? Why—I don't know what you're talking about."

"I can read," retorted the bandit. "And they print newspapers. You gave out an interview in St. Louis——"

"Jeff," began Ferdinand Barat. "I didn't want to come out here——"

"All right," snapped his brother. "We lose a trick. We'll win the next. Give him the money you've got with you."

Ferdinand Barat opened his waistcoat, reached under his broadcloth shirt and brought out a thick money belt. He shoved it beside the gunny sack.

"There's ten thousand dollars in that," he said grimly.

"A day's profit in the stock market," replied the bandit.

He picked up the money belt and the sack. But before he backed away his eyes stared again at Bonniwell. Bonniwell remained impassive. Every cent of money he had in the world was going away with the train robber, but he made no protest.

The bandits did not molest any of the other passengers, a fact on which Jeff Barat commented. "They stopped the train for just that ten thousand——"

The bandits backed out of the end of the car and slammed the door. Woeltjen yanked out his gun then and began pushing away from the table. "Let me out. Mebbe I can get a shot——!"

There was a rattle of gunfire outside the train, then the drumming of horses' hoofs.

"No use," said Jeff Barat.

His brother began to curse. He did it well for a man from the East. "For that you brought me out to this damned wilderness——"

"Easy, Ferd," snapped Jeff Barat. "What's ten thousand to what you'll make out of this country?"

"Lucky I'm going to Baker, instead of away," said Pearson, the cattleman.

"You've a herd coming to Baker?" Jeff Barat asked.

Pearson nodded. "Six thousand head. My foreman's handling the drive. I took a Morgan ship to New Orleans, then came upriver. Thought I'd go direct to Chicago and make a dicker with the packers. Found they're all here in Kansas, doing their buying at railhead."

"Your herd's coming to Baker, Mr. Pearson?" Jeff Barat asked. "Like to talk to you about it."

"Jesse James!" someone in the car yelled. "The James gang, that's who they was."

"Ah, hell!" snarled Woeltjen. "Every damn holdup in

this country is laid to the Jameses. Me, I don't know of no one who ever even saw the James boys."

"This is their country," remarked Jeff Barat. "I wonder——" He looked at Bonniwell.

Bonniwell returned Barat's look steadily. After a moment he got up. "As I've no more money to continue playing, I guess I'll get some sleep."

"Goin' a long way?" asked Barat.

"Not very far."

There was a question in Barat's eyes, but Bonniwell did not answer it. He went on to his own seat. Someone had appropriated the seat he had occupied by the window. A woman. Bonniwell looked down at her.

She was not like the expensively dressed women on the train. She was as beautiful as any of them; her clothes were as good. Yet she was not rouged. And she did not have the same expression.

She saw him looking down, flushed, then looked up at the baggage rack.

"Oh!" she exclaimed. "Did I take your seat?"

"Not at all," said Bonniwell. "I shouldn't have left." He looked quickly up the aisle, saw no other vacant seats than the one beside her.

He sat down. He was embarrassed. He always was in the presence of women. Even with Eleanor Simmons he had never become entirely at ease.

He sat in silence for a moment. Then the girl spoke. "Do you suppose that was really the notorious Jesse James?"

"Yes," he replied. "And the big man was Cole Younger."

"How do you know?" she exclaimed.

"I met a man once who had a quiet voice and blue eyes," said Bonniwell. "He didn't say he was Jesse James, but he didn't deny it."

"But didn't he take your money?"

"Every cent I had."

"There were only two of them," she said, then caught herself. "Oh, but of course! You're not armed."

"If I had been I wouldn't have drawn against Jesse, with his gun on me. Not for mere money."

She looked at him. "You've been in this country before, haven't you?"

"Several years. Since the war."

"I'm from Illinois. Oh, I forgot. My name's Lou Sager. I'm going to Baker."

"Baker? You've relatives there?"

"No. Not at all. I read in a newspaper that the city is booming and so I—well, I thought it offered an opportunity to me."

"Baker isn't a city," said Bonniwell. "It's a little town of about 600 population."

"Oh, but that article I read said the population was around 5,000!"

"The paper was right, and it wasn't," said Bonniwell. "Baker's a trail town."

Her smooth white forehead creased. "A trail town? What do you mean?"

"It's on the Chisholm Trail. In winter it has a population of 600. But during the cattle season it swells to four and five thousand population. It's a wild place."

"Yes, I read that in the paper. That's why I'm going there. The article said that these cattlemen who come to Baker sell their stock for enormous prices and spend practically all their money right away, mostly on luxuries they take back to Texas with them. I understand their women get really few up-to-date clothes, hats for example——"

"Hats?" Bonniwell asked blankly.

She smiled. "I'm a milliner. The Texas men spend huge amounts for their—what do they call them, ten-gallon hats? Isn't it natural then they'd want to buy fine hats for their women to take home? That's what I thought. So I'm going to Baker to open a millinery shop."

"Oh, Lord!" said John Bonniwell under his breath.

"Did you say something?"

"Yes. Did you talk that plan over with anyone before you started out for here?"

"Just my mother. She's in Springfield, Illinois. I had a little store there, but it wasn't doing very well. So I sold it out and decided to try out here where the country is booming. I intend to send for mother when I get established."

Bonniwell drew a deep breath. "Miss, I was in Baker last year. It was *hell!*"

She looked startled. "I don't understand!"

"No. You don't. Or you wouldn't have come out here. Baker is a wild place. Twenty-two men were killed there last year. How many this year, I don't know. Gunfights are almost hourly occurrences."

"Oh," she scoffed. "I've heard of all that. I believe it's greatly exaggerated. Granted that these frontier cities are wild, surely no one would *shoot* a woman."

"You've never met a Texas man," said Bonniwell soberly. "In his home country he's a desirable citizen. But every Texas man is a gunman. He's raised with a gun. It takes months to drive a herd of cattle to Trail Town. During that time the herders see no women, no civilized communities. They get lonesome, vicious. Then they reach a trail town, and receive a year's wages. They try to spend it as quickly as possible. On liquor, other things. They raise hell, Miss!"

For a full moment she looked at him, her eyes wide, then she blinked. "You're painting a rather black picture. I've always heard Southerners were chivalrous, courteous gentlemen——"

"The Texas gentlemen stay at home. The Texas men who come with the herds are not planters. They're cattle men. You'll see. We reach Baker in a half hour."

The Barats, Bonniwell saw, were also getting off at Baker. Bonniwell helped Lou Sager with her carpetbag. He saw her worried look as she got off the train and looked out across the town.

"It—doesn't look very cheerful, does it?" she asked doubtfully.

Bonniwell looked up the dusty street. He saw the flimsy buildings jammed side by side on both sides of the street. He saw swirling crowds of men—and he heard the banging of guns.

"I think," he said, "Baker is treed!"

Chapter Three

TRAIL TOWN

BY THE TIME they got the Pearson herd into the wide roadway that was the Chisholm Trail, the cowboys with the drive were on fairly good terms. Each cowboy knew the stature and mettle of the other. They'd had their squabbles while rounding up the wild steers.

Clem Hawks, the foreman, was satisfied with his riders. If any bunch could push a herd of three thousand wild Longhorns up the nine-hundred-mile trail, this bunch could.

Hawks had been up the trail four times before. He'd been to Abilene twice, Caldwell once and Wichita once. This time he was headed for Baker, Kansas. His previous trips had been hard. They had taxed his strength to the limit.

The four trips combined had been as a picnic compared to this, the fifth. Two days north of Austin the herd stampeded.

It took three full days to get it back on the trail. Then, by count, there were sixty head more than there should have been. Hawks let the extras stay with the herd.

The Salt Fork River was a roaring torrent, a half mile wide and full of driftwood. The lead steers refused to enter the water. Hawks and a couple of men waded their horses deep into the river, while some of the other cowboys tried by might and main to get the leaders of the herd into the water. They balked every time.

They had to give it up. A thunderstorm started up shortly after dark, and men spent the entire night in frantic endeavor to prevent the herd from stampeding again. The river was impassable the next morning. Not until the third day were they able to get across.

The Cimarron was at flood stage and it took two days to cross it. The cattle stampeded four times during the next week and Hawks ordered the men to shoot the half dozen leaders, knowing that animals sometimes get the stampede habit and never lose it.

Comanches, even though bribed with several steers, harried the herd. Twice the Pearson cowboys had to drive the Indians off with guns.

By the time they neared the Kansas line the fourteen cowboys with the Pearson steers scarcely spoke to one another. Then one evening Jim Malachy rode into the camp on a spent bronc.

He was whiskered and gaunt, ragged and dirty from a hard trip. Only his guns were in good condition.

"Howdy, Clem," he greeted the foreman as he hunkered down by the campfire.

Clem Hawks regarded him sourly. "The only other trouble we needed was you, Malachy. Who'd you kill in Texas?"

"Nobody much," replied Malachy. "Just an ornery deputy who tried to arrest me."

Hawks grunted. "You'll never be an old man, Malachy."

"Don't want to be," Malachy chuckled. "When do we reach town, Clem? Want to see if they're as much fun as the boys say they are."

Hawks blinked. "They don't stand for hurrahing up here any more."

"The hell you say, Hawks. Why, the Brown outfit's braggin' all over Victoria County how they got two peace marshals last fall. You goin' to let the folks at home think the Browns are a better outfit than the Pearsons?"

"Stop that kind o' talk, Malachy!" snapped Hawks. "We've had enough trouble on this trip, 'thout lettin' any of the boys stay up here in Boot Hill."

Malachy rose to his feet and grinned down on Clem Hawks.

"Just as you say, Clem," he said. He moved away from the fire and went around to the cowboys, most of whom he knew. They knew him, too—the worst of the Malachy boys.

Malachy was good for the morale of the cowboys, however. Hawks had to admit that a couple of days later. He did practically no work, but the cowboys stopped quarreling and fighting among themselves. They were much too interested in listening to Malachy.

He told good stories. During the war, he'd been a captain under McCulloch during the early Missouri campaigns. Later he'd been transferred to the Army of Northern Virginia and had commanded a regiment at Winchester. He was with Lee at Appomattox Court House.

And then he had returned to Texas to find the large Malachy family land- and cattle-rich and money-poor.

He went to New Orleans and learned the vocation of gambling. He killed a man at Natchez and returned to Texas. He bought a couple of horses and raced them for a season or two. In East Texas a disgruntled loser accused him of doping a horse. Naturally, Malachy killed him. He had to leave so quickly he left his race horses behind. He visited with relatives throughout the state, got into gambling scrapes and shot a man or two. There were several warrants out for his arrest, but around Austin, his home territory, he was reasonably safe. Until now.

So he was finally "going north." And it was the ill fortune of Clem Hawks to get him along with his trail herd.

Well, Hawks' own responsibility would soon be over. Mr. Pearson would meet him at Baker and the herd would no doubt be sold shortly thereafter. In the meantime he was keeping the boys entertained with his wild stories.

Nine days into Kansas and Clem Hawks made final camp.

"We're twenty miles from Baker," he told the cowboys. "We stay here until Mr. Pearson sells the herd, then we drive it to town."

"Twenty miles from Baker!" exclaimed Pete Youmans. "Hell, I thought we were going right to town."

"We've got to keep the herd together," said Hawks. "I can only let four of you go at a time."

It didn't take the lucky four more than five minutes to get ready. Jim Malachy prepared to go with them. Clem Hawks watched him with a brooding eye.

"You're not under my orders, Malachy," Hawks said, "but the rest of you are. Remember, you get into trouble, you get out by yourselves." He was lying and the boys knew it. Hawks would go to the last ditch for his boys.

They raced away from the camp, the four cowboys and Jim Malachy.

Three hours later they came to the toll bridge, on the other side of which was Baker. They could see the lights of it and hear the noise. They were impatient to get to it. A watchman stepepd into the middle of the bridge and said:

"Two bits apiece, boys."

Jim Malachy yanked out a Frontier Model and sent a bullet past the watchman's hat. The four cowboys promptly spurred their horses. The watchman had to jump aside to keep from being ridden down.

"Here she is, boys!" cried Jim Malachy. "Our town! Let's see what makes her tick."

They had no trouble finding the Longhorn Saloon, even though it was already dark. It was the biggest saloon on Main Street, having a dance hall in connection.

They tied their horses outside the saloon and stamped in, ragged and dirty and wild. The saloon was jammed with more than a hundred men. The moment he stepped inside, Jim Malachy drew his guns and fired two shots into the ceiling.

"The Pearson outfit's just in from Texas!" he roared.

"Yip-ee!" yelled the four cowboys with him.

Instantly a man with a badge on his vest stepped over to them.

"Where do you think you're at?" he snapped.

"In Kansas," retorted Jim Malachy. "You want to make somethin' of it?"

"I do," said the marshal. "Hand over them guns. You ain't shootin' up this town."

The four cowboys looked to Malachy for leadership. The good humor left the Texas killer's face.

"My name's Jim Malachy," he said, "I never gave my guns to anyone. You want to *take* them?"

With Malachy's speech the cowboys behind him stiffened. The marshal looked at them, hesitated and was lost.

"All right," he said. "But take things easy."

The five Texas men brushed the lawman aside and marched to the bar.

"Whisky!" roared Jim Malachy. "Quarts of it. The Pearson outfit's drinkin'!"

There were nine Texas men to every Kansan in the saloon. Inside of five minutes the place was in an uproar. The newcomers had defied the law and got away with it. The Texans who were already here and had been behaving reasonably well threw off all restraint.

The marshal slipped out of the saloon. He did not reappear that evening. The town of Baker belonged to the Texans that night. They drank and caroused and whooped it up until dawn. Then some of them rode out to their camps on the near-by prairie. Others settled down here and there to sleep.

But not the Pearson cowboys. Somehow they attached a group to them and went from saloon to saloon. When their money ran out they chased the bartenders from behind the bars and helped themselves to liquor. One bartender pulled a shotgun from under the bar and they took it away from him and clubbed him insensible.

They wrecked a restaurant at seven in the morning because the proprietor claimed he didn't have enough eggs and ham to feed them all.

At nine o'clock Mayor Olcott cornered his law enforcement body, consisting of a marshal and two deputies, and issued orders to drive the drunken Texans from Baker.

The marshal remembered seeing a notice in the sheriff's office about one Jim Malachy, wanted in Texas, and passed the buck to the sheriff.

"He's your man, Stengel," he said. "There's five hundred reward for his scalp and I wouldn't do you out of it."

"The hell you wouldn't," snarled the sheriff. He stormed about his office, biting his mustache; then he took off his two gunbelts and hung them up on a nail.

He drew one of the guns from its holster and stuck the gun into the waistband of his trousers. After that he got his coat and put it on, buttoning it tightly. It completely concealed the gun in his waistband.

"Gonna take him by guile?" asked the marshal sarcastically.

The sheriff cursed.

"I don't know why I ever quit the bone pickin' business," he said. He went out of his office, slamming the door.

It was easy enough to find Malachy. There were still fifty Texas men with him and they hadn't quieted any since the evening before.

They were in the Cimarron Saloon. Sheriff Stengel went in and worked his way quietly to the bar. It was five minutes before Malachy noticed him.

"Who the hell are you?" he demanded then.

Sheriff Stengel shrugged. "You're Jud Pearson's cousin, aren't you?"

"What if I am?"

"Nothin'. Except Jud telegraphed me that you were comin'. Said to tell you everything's fixed in Texas."

"How'd Jud know I was here?"

"I wouldn't know. I got his telegram here——"

Sheriff Stengel slipped his hand under his coat lapels, persumably reaching for the telegram. His hand came out—with the Frontier Model Colt. The muzzle of it jammed into Jim Malachy's stomach.

"Here's the telegram!" the sheriff snarled. "And any o' your herd try anythin', you get it first, Malachy, right through the guts!"

The cowboys almost lifted the roof with their roar. Guns flashed, but no one came close to the sheriff and Malachy. The boys had been out with the killer all night. They had recognized him as their leader and they would not now jeopardize his life.

Malachy grinned feebly. "Guess you got me, sheriff."

"You guess right. Hand me your guns, butt first."

Malachy made an elaborate show of drawing his weapons from their holsters. He tendered them butt first to the sheriff. The sheriff reached for them—and Baker saw, for the first time, the spin that was to become famous in later years. Malachy kept his forefingers in the trigger guards of the pistols. As he held the guns out butt first, he made a quick, almost imperceptible movement and the guns twirled completely around, so the muzzles were pointing forward instead of the butts. At the instant the butts slapped into Malachy's palms, his hands contracted and the guns thundered.

The sheriff was dead before he hit the floor of the saloon.

John Bonniwell looked down the main street. A couple of blocks away he saw a moving knot of men. He saw puffs of smoke billowing out from among them; he heard the banging of guns.

He scooped up Lou Sager's bag, tucked it under his left arm, then picked up his own with the same hand. With his other hand he caught her arm. "We'd better get off the street. Trouble's coming our way."

He led her hurriedly to the express office, a half block away. In their wake trailed the Barat Brothers and two or three other passengers, who had, to their sorrow, alighted from the train at Baker.

A man was peeking out of the door of the express office.

"What's all the shooting about?" Bonniwell asked.

"Jim Malachy," exclaimed the agent. "He killed the sheriff this morning. Judge Atwater acquitted him because the sheriff drew first. The mayor objected and Malachy felt insulted. He and his gang began shooting up the town a couple of hours ago. Looks like it'll be treed for the rest of the summer."

"Haven't you got a town marshal?" Bonniwell asked.

The express agent snorted. "Three. They remembered they had private business somewhere. Law's what Baker ain't got today." Well, it was none of John Bonniwell's affair. He carried his and Lou Sager's bags into the building.

"Mr. Wells," said a voice. "John Wells!"

There were eight or nine persons in the room, four of them women. Bonniwell saw only one, though.

"Miss Simmons!" he exclaimed. "How did you come here?"

Eleanor Simmons held out her hand to Bonniwell. This *is* a surprise!" She was smiling radiantly, and John Bonniwell's nostrils flared as he looked into her flushed face.

"You knew I was coming here. Remember? I'm going to visit my uncle Oliver in Broken Lance. I'm on my way there now."

"How long've you been here?" he asked inanely.

"Since yesterday."

"But why'd you stay over? Baker's no place——"

The express agent was inside, now, putting thick, wooden shutters over the windows.

"Stage didn't run yesterday," he said. "Bandits held it up, killed the driver."

"But where'd you stay overnight?" Bonniwell persisted.

"Why, at the Baker Hotel. Of course, it's not the Planters Hotel. But still——"

The Baker Hotel. Thin, boarded walls, cubbyholes above the roaring Baker Saloon and Dance Hall. Eleanor Simmons had remained there overnight. Bonniwell shook his head. Then he turned to the express agent, who was dropping a bar across the door.

"The stage is leaving today, isn't it?"

"Maybe," snorted the agent. "If those damned Texas men will let it."

Someone banged against the door.

"Lemme in!" cried a frightened voice. "Lemme in."

"There's enough people in here now," cried the agent.

"Lemme in!" repeated the frantic voice outside. "Damn you, lemme in. This is Olcott, the mayor!"

Bonniwell stepped to the door and raised the wooden bar. A short, paunchy man fell into the little office. A bullet kicked up dirt at his heels. Olcott howled and leaped behind the stove.

"Close the door, you!" cried the agent from behind the sheet iron stove.

Bonniwell reached to close the door, and a bullet grazed his coat sleeve and slammed into the partly closed door. He stepped away.

"Come on out of there, Olcott!" yelled a raucous voice.

A woman behind Bonniwell moaned. He knew that it wasn't either Eleanor Simmons or Lou Sager. He turned and surveyed the persons in the room. Jeff Barat was leaning carelessly against the wall—on the safe side. His brother was trying to cower behind Jeff's slenderer figure.

"What's the matter with your law, Mayor?" Bonniwell asked.

Olcott cursed loudly. "Stengel is dead and the damned marshals are hiding. The yellow rats!"

"Come on out, Olcott," yelled the voice out on the street. "Come out or we'll come get you. And we'll come shootin'!"

"Go on, get outside!" snarled the express agent. "You're the mayor." He shoved the fat little mayor.

Olcott howled and wrestled with the agent. The agent hit him in the face and the mayor went sprawling to the dirt floor.

"Cut it, you two!" snapped Bonniwell. "Isn't it bad enough without you fighting in here? Olcott, you'd better go out. There're women here. If Malachy and his gang come in to get you, the women'll get hurt."

"I don't go outside," yelled Olcott. "Go out yourself."

"I'm not a city official," retorted Bonniwell. "I'm just a customer waiting for the stage."

"Then keep your mouth shut! You ain't even got a gun. What's the matter, you afraid to carry one?"

Several bullets smashed into the front of the express office. The yells on the street became a chorus. "We're coming, Olcott! And we're comin' shootin'!"

Bonniwell looked around the circle of drawn faces. Four women. If the Texas men came in shooting, the women stood an excellent chance of being killed, even though the Texans might suddenly become chivalrous and try to keep their bullets only for Olcott.

Bonniwell stooped and tore open his carpetbag. He whipped out a long, Frontier Model Colt. He spun the cylinder and stuck the gun in the waistband of his trousers.

Then he stepped out of the office.

In the middle of the dusty street was a clump of wild-eyed, drunken Texans. There were at least twenty of them, all armed. John Bonniwell faced them, his hands hanging loosely at his sides.

He picked out the leader of the mob, a gaunt, black-bearded man, who had a Colt in each hand.

"You!" Blackbeard roared. "Who're you?"

Bonniwell said, "Drop those guns, Jim Malachy!"

Malachy was forty feet from Bonniwell, but Bonniwell

could see the Texan blink in astonishment. He saw, too, the rise of Malachy's shoulders and knew that those guns were coming up in a second—and would spout!

For Bonniwell to draw meant death. Death for himself and some of those in the express office behind him. Yet the only thing he could do was draw.

"Bonniwell!" cried a voice behind Malachy. "It's John Bonniwell!"

Bonniwell saw the shudder that ran through Jim Malachy; he was aware that the men behind the black-bearded Texan were suddenly shuffling. They knew him now. But they were twenty to one.

He kept his eyes on Jim Malachy's right hand. He saw the hand move up an inch, stop.

Among men of guns, news of men with guns travels far. Even in Texas Malachy had heard of John Bonniwell.

"Bonniwell," he said hoarsely. "I thought you were dead!"

"*You* will be," replied Bonniwell, "if you don't drop those guns at once."

Malachy stared at Bonniwell. He could see that the lean man wore no holsters, that he had only the one .45 stuck in his waistband, an awkward place from which to draw.

And Malachy had two guns in his hands and his followers all had their own weapons ready. They could kill Bonniwell, a feat that would earn them homage up and down the length of the Chisholm Trail.

But Malachy knew, too, that he could not kill Bonniwell before Bonniwell got that gun out of his waistband and fired at least once. And Malachy knew where the one bullet would land.

Jim Malachy let his guns fall to the dust.

John Bonniwell's hands remained at his sides.

"You're smart, Jim," he said. "You'll be smarter, though, if you tell your men to drop *their* guns. There's women back there in the stage office and you wouldn't want to see them get hurt, would you?"

"No," said Jim Malachy. He half turned his head. "Boys, do as John Bonniwell says."

And they did!

Twenty men dropped their guns to the street. They wouldn't have done that for any other man in the West except John Bonniwell.

Bonniwell heard the thump of feet behind him. He said,

without turning, "Get a sack and gather up those guns. Take them to Malachy's camp—later."

"John Bonniwell!" said the voice of Olcott, the mayor of Baker. "You're Bonniwell." He came up beside Bonniwell, his eyes bulging in awe.

Bonniwell kept his gaze on the Texas men.

"Get those guns, Olcott!" he ordered. "Get them before they change their minds."

The Texas men weren't changing their minds, though. Not today. They were retreating across the street. Bonniwell watched until Olcott had gathered up the last gun, then he turned abruptly and went back into the express office.

The agent and two or three of the others had come out. They stared at Bonniwell. He did not look at them. He stepped inside the little room and looked at Eleanor Simmons.

She had come from behind the stove, stood beside it. And her face was dead. Her eyes were wide and unblinking.

"You're John Bonniwell," she said tonelessly. "You're the man we talked about in the hospital. The Haleyville gunfighter who killed all those men."

"Yes," he admitted in a low voice. "I changed my name because of the newspapers. They wouldn't——"

"John Bonniwell," Eleanor went on, not seeming to hear him. "You're the man the newspapers said was the most notorious killer in the entire West."

He said evenly: "I have never killed anyone who didn't need killing, who didn't try to kill me first."

Lou Sager, at one side, could contain herself no longer. "You just saw what he did! He saved our lives. Are you condemning the man for that?"

"No," said Eleanor Simmons. "I'm not condemning him for anything. Perhaps . . . in this country . . . the John Bonniwells are necessary. But I—his hands are red—red with the blood of men he's killed."

Eleanor Simmons laughed hysterically. "Why, when I went back to Illinois from St. Louis I saw some boys playing a game. I heard them. They were quarreling. They all wanted to be John Bonniwell. Bonniwell the killer!"

Bonniwell turned abruptly and walked out of the express office.

"Bonniwell!" cried Olcott, the mayor. "You're the man I've been waiting for. I want you to be marshal of Baker. I'll pay you two hundred and fifty dollars a month."

Bonniwell walked past him.

"Four hundred!" cried the mayor. "And three dollars for every arrest you make."

Bonniwell walked up the street. But already the word had gone ahead of him. It had leaped from mouth to mouth, from saloon to saloon.

"Bonniwell's here. John Bonniwell's alive and he's here!"

The fight in Haleyville last year had been national news. In the West it had been a tremendous sensation. Bonniwell against four men, every one a notorious gunfighter. He'd killed all of them. He had been riddled with bullets himself, so badly wounded word had gone around that he couldn't live. Then he had disappeared and after a while men said that he was dead. Law officers had buried him and wanted to keep it a secret.

John Bonniwell became a legend. For six months men had believed him dead. He had gone out in a blaze of glory. And now—now he had come back as spectacularly as he had gone.

The curse of John Bonniwell was that everything he did was spectacular.

Chapter Four

LEAD FOR HIRE

WHEN BONNIWELL entered the Baker Hotel he was given the best room in the house, a corner one, overlooking the street, but on the side opposite from where the dance hall was below. The quiet side.

He went upstairs and took out two cartridge belts from his carpetbag. The other Frontier Model Colt with the eight inch barrels, too.

The die was cast. He'd been recognized in Baker. They knew he was back. From now on his life was in continual danger. There were Texas men who remembered him from Haleyville. And here in Baker were Jim Malachy and his crew. He had won a victory over them, but that didn't mean they'd remain cowed. Liquor breeds courage in some men.

Bonniwell didn't mind brave men so much. It was the others, the ones deathly afraid of him that he feared. Such men would shoot on slight provocation, perhaps no provocation at all. And they might not always give proper warning. A dark spot, a turned back was often enough incentive.

There was brackish water in a cracked pitcher. He poured some of it into a thick china basin and washed his hands and face.

Then he put on a clean white shirt and strapped both cartridge belts around his waist. He tested the actions of the Colts, saw they were loaded, five shells in each, an empty chamber under the hammer.

He had to show himself in Baker. You had to show yourself after a victory, otherwise men might believe that reaction had set in and you were afraid. He buckled gun belts about his waist.

He came out of the hotel, stood in front of the place for a few minutes. Then he began a deliberate stroll along the wooden sidewalk that bordered the east side of the street. He walked two blocks, to the railroad depot, then crossed to the west side of the street and walked back. No one talked to him during the entire trip, yet every man looked at him and knew him.

After he finished his tour he looked at his watch, a heavy gold piece, and found it was almost six o'clock. He saw a sign: "Good Eats" and turned in.

There was a counter inside, also a half dozen tables with checkered cloths. He sat down at one of the tables, carelessly choosing the side where his back would be against the wall.

A pert looking girl in a gingham dress came to take his order. He asked for beefsteak and fried potatoes and the girl went to the kitchen.

He put his elbows on the table and watched the street outside. After a minute he inhaled sharply. A man had stopped before the window, was peering in. He saw Bonniwell and slammed open the door.

"John!" he cried.

Bonniwell got to his feet. "Tom," he said.

They shook hands and held the grip just a bit longer than was necessary. Then Tom Waggoner sat down opposite Bonniwell. "I just heard a few minutes ago that you were— alive."

Warmth flooded through Bonniwell. This man was his

closest friend, the only man he would have trusted to watch his back in a gun battle, though Waggoner wasn't a gunfighter.

"You were in Colorado, Tom," he said.

"Yes. I heard about it two weeks after it happened. But the paper said you were killed. When I got to Haleyville the Texas men owned the town. No one seemed to know anything about you. And then I had to go on another surveying trip. Where were you, John?"

"St. Louis. All winter. I just got off this damned train here this afternoon."

"I know. The town's buzzing."

"How're they taking it?"

Waggoner shrugged. "With plenty of liquor. It sticks in their throats. Malachy realizes now he lost face. John, I'm taking another trip. Why don't you come along?"

Bonniwell smiled wanly. "If you'll wait a couple of days."

Waggoner sighed. "All right, I'll wait, but I'd rather go now. I know how you are. But, John, I'm glad you're back. Have you any plans?"

"Nary a plan. I thought some of going to Texas and raising cattle, but I guess I just couldn't get along with Texas folks."

Waggoner chuckled. "Not unless you change your name."

The waitress brought Bonniwell's food and Waggoner ordered a similar portion for himself. When the girl had gone again Waggoner said, "John, I'm headed for a place called Broken Lance. Do you know it?"

Bonniwell looked sharply at Waggoner. "Yes, I've heard about it."

"Come with me to Broken Lance. I'm going there to do some building for the railroad."

"Is it going to touch Broken Lance?"

"Yes. That's what I wanted to tell you about. They're building now. The road will be there inside of thirty days. It's going due West. West, not southwest. Do you know what that means?"

Bonniwell considered for a moment. "Why, it will be the closest railroad point to Texas, won't it?"

"Exactly, and from now on Broken Lance will be trail's end for all herds. I happen to know there won't be a road going down into Texas for four or five years, at least. Do you know what that's going to do for Broken Lance? It's going to make it a city. A Wichita, a Dodge and a Baker, all rolled into one. Only it will be more permanent."

The door of the restaurant opened and Lou Sager looked in timidly. Bonniwell saw her and pushed back his chair.

"Miss Sager!" he called.

She saw him and smiled in obvious relief. She came into the restaurant.

"Will you have a seat with us?" he asked.

She looked doubtful. "Is it all right?"

"Oh, yes. This is Tom Waggoner, my friend."

Waggoner bowed. He did it well. Bonniwell knew that he was a Harvard man and came from a fine family. Waggoner's eyes sparkled as he looked at Lou Sager. "You're the milliner, aren't you?"

She was surprised. "Why, how did you know—through Mr. Bonniwell?"

Waggoner grinned boyishly. "Miss Sager, everyone knew all about you ten minutes after you got off the train. Well, how do you like it here?"

Bonniwell saw the little crease in her otherwise smooth forehead. "It's not exactly what I expected."

"I told you about it on the train, Miss Sager," Bonniwell said softly. "It can be even worse than you saw it today. Why don't you go back?"

She shook her head quickly, "Oh, I couldn't do that. I—I've burned my bridges."

Bonniwell sighed lightly. "Tom, would I be violating any confidence if I told Miss Sager about Broken Lance?"

"No, not in this case."

So Bonniwell told her about the future of Broken Lance, finishing with, "Baker will be dead in a month. If you started a store here, you'd be ruined. If you must stay out here, Broken Lance is the place to go. Although I'm warning you, the town will be as bad as this one—worse, probably, because there will be more of it."

"You're going there, Mr. Bonniwell?" she asked.

Waggoner answered for Bonniwell. "Yes. And so am I."

The three of them ate their dinners, and then Bonniwell realized with astonishment that he didn't have a dollar in the world. He had checked into the hotel and come into the restaurant without even realizing he was broke.

Bonniwell led Waggoner to one side.

"Tom, I'm flat," he said. "Have you got any money?"

"Of course. How much do you want? I've got a thousand with me and around five thousand to my credit on the railroad's books."

"Let me have five hundred. I want to continue a game I was in with Jeff Barat on the train."

Waggoner scowled. "So he's around again."

Bonniwell nodded. "He's brought a brother with him. Seems to be an Eastern capitalist big enough for the Missouri Boys to stop the train. They got ten thousand from him."

"The Missouri Boys, eh?"

"They were masked, but I recognized Jesse and Cole Younger. I contributed my own stake."

"They must have caught you unawares."

"Not exactly, Tom. I didn't have my guns, but if I had I wouldn't have pulled them—not for a few hundred dollars. I don't think you know Jesse. I met him a year ago. There isn't a man in the West can pull a gun against him. Not that he's so fast, but just because he's the most desperate man in the country. They've been after him so long he's gun-shy. He'd kill a man who'd snap his fingers unexpectedly."

Tom Waggoner rubbed his smooth shaven chin with the back of his hand. "I didn't know he was in Kansas. There's some money going down on the stage tomorrow. We're building a depot, freight buildings and some pretty large loading pens in Broken Lance."

"Better get yourself a good man to ride shotgun."

"How about you, John? As long as you're going to Broken Lance, anyway."

During the long winter in St. Louis, Bonniwell had decided that he would never again engage in any work that required the use of a gun. But he couldn't turn down Tom Waggoner. He nodded. "All right, Tom."

They sat in the hotel lobby talking for an hour. Men came in and went to the saloon and dance hall. Soon the noise was so great that Bonniwell and Waggoner could scarcely hear each other.

Finally, the Barat brothers came down the stairs.

The older one was resplendent in Prince Albert and shining silk hat. Jeff Barat wore a Prince Albert, too, but his had a velvet collar and more of his starched cuffs showed at the wrists.

Jeff Barat said to Bonniwell, "That was good work this afternoon. I was sure I had seen you before."

"Jeff has told me about you, Mr. Bonniwell," the older Barat said. "Your name was mentioned in New York by Ned Buntline."

"Oh, yes," said Bonniwell. "He was in Haleyville last year. This is Mr. Waggoner."

Bonniwell looked blandly at Jeff Barat. "Too bad you lost all your loose change. I was hoping we might continue that game."

Jeff Barat showed his white teeth. "They were in a little too much of a hurry. Ferd had most of his roll in his boots."

He smiled pleasantly. "Gambling's my business, you know. What are we waiting for?"

"Not a thing," replied Bonniwell.

They walked into the saloon and the bartender seated them at a corner table. He brought cards. Jeff Barat pushed the deck to Bonniwell. "What'll it be? The same?"

Bonniwell nodded. He brought out the five hundred dollars he had just borrowed. Tom Waggoner brought out his own roll, a few dollars more than five hundred. Bonniwell looked with satisfaction at the size of the bills Ferd Barat brought out. Bonniwell dealt the cards around. Jeff Barat looked at his and said, "By the way, Mr. Bonniwell, do you suppose that was really Jesse James?"

Bonniwell shrugged. "Yes, it was. And the big man was Cole Younger."

"You've seen them before?"

"In Haleyville last year. They stopped off a couple of days."

Jeff Barat sighed heavily. "That fellow's luck is about due to run out. He's been at it a long time. I'm thinking I'd like to meet him again when the breaks aren't all on his side."

"Not me," said Bonniwell. "He's dangerous." He was looking past Jeff Barat and smiled suddenly.

"Hello, John," said a man. He was a tall, well-built young fellow, almost a boy, except for his serious, rather old expression.

"Hello, Bat," said Bonniwell. "How's things in Dodge?"

The young man shook hands with Bonniwell. Bonniwell turned to the others. "This is Bat Masterson, Mr. Waggoner, Mr. Jeff Barat, and Mr. Ferdinand Barat."

The others at the table shook hands with young Bat Masterson. Jeff Barat seemed particularly interested. "Heard a lot about you," he said. "Somehow I figgered you was an older man."

"I'm eighteen," said Bat Masterson.

"My friend Ned Buntline spoke about you," offered Ferdinand Barat.

Bat Masterson's eyes lit up. "He tell you about the buffalo hunt last year?"

"I don't recall it exactly. Seems I recollect that he talked mostly of hunting men. Bad men."

"How about sitting in, Mr. Masterson?" Jeff Barat asked.

"Why, sure, I'd like to."

Masterson, despite his youth, had been around. He was a good poker player, one of the best Bonniwell had ever met. Jeff Barat played his usual cold, merciless game. If Bonniwell had been matched only against Masterson and Jeff Barat, things would not have gone well with him. But the older Barat and Tom Waggoner, to a certain extent, offset the efficiency of the professional gambler and the young buffalo hunter. Bonniwell won slowly but steadily. At the end of four hours of playing, when the game broke up, he was ahead eight hundred dollars. Waggoner had lost about two hundred. Masterson and Jeff Barat were both big winners, the older Barat having contributed a large share of the losses.

"Sorry we can't play tomorrow," said Jeff Barat, "but we're leaving on the morning stage for Broken Lance."

"So are we," said Tom Waggoner. "John is going to ride shotgun."

Jeff Barat's eyes slitted. "How long are you going to stay there?" he asked, looking at Bonniwell.

Bonniwell shrugged. "I don't know." But he just remembered something—something he had forgotten when he had promised Tom Waggoner that he would ride shotgun.

The stage hadn't gone today. That meant Eleanor Simmons was still in Baker, due to go southwest tomorrow. She would be in the stagecoach. Bonniwell's eyes clouded at the thought.

Chapter Five

AMBUSH

THAT PART OF BAKER which was not sleeping it off from the night before was gathered around the stagecoach office at ten o'clock, the time scheduled for the stage to depart. Billy Coogan was the driver. He was already up on the box trying to hold in his six-horse team. Tom Waggoner was beside him. In the coach the two Barat brothers had made themselves comfortable. There was another man with them, a man wearing a long, black coat, a flat-crowned black hat and a white collar turned backwards. He had a meek looking face, but his eyes were bright. He was the Reverend James Fellows. Bonniwell sat on the top of the stagecoach, his legs dangling over the loaded boot. His two Frontier Models were conspicuous. Beside him lay a short double-barreled shotgun and across his knees a .45-75 Winchester rifle. He was really armed.

"I'm all ready!" Billy Coogan called down to the express agent.

"Two more passengers," said the agent. "Here they come."

Bonniwell did not turn his head. He did not see them until they were directly under him, entering the coach. Lou Sager spoke to him then. "Good morning, Mr. Bonniwell."

Bonniwell looked down. "Morning, Miss Sager." And then his eyes met the upturned face of Eleanor Simmons.

She looked at him for a full second and then, without a sign of recognition, got up into the coach.

"Let her roll!" yelled the agent.

Billy Coogan started to crack his long whip, but before it snapped the six-horse team was leaping away. They were off—for Broken Lance, a hundred miles to the southwest. Trail's end.

It took a person with a strong constitution to make an extended stagecoach trip. The trail that served for a road was rutted. When there was a hole or a boulder the road swerved sharply out. The horses never slackened for any detour. They traveled at almost a continuous gallop. The coach swayed and jounced the passengers all around. It was fortunate that they had to change horses every few hours.

The first change was made so quickly that the passengers scarcely got time to relax. The man in charge of the horse station had the fresh team waiting, already harnessed. It was only a minute's work to unhitch the tired horses and substitute the fresh, and then they were off again.

Shortly after two the stage rolled into another station and Billy Coogan announced, "Half hour for lunch, folks."

Everyone got off the coach and went into the cabin. Plates and food were already on the table and they ate quickly. There was still ten minutes left when Bonniwell and Waggoner went outside.

"Another hour or two and I think we'll be all right, John," Waggoner said.

Bonniwell nodded. "Yes, I think if they are going to make any attempt they'll make it soon."

Lou Sager came out of the station. Bonniwell walked over to her. She looked at him, worried. "Mr. Bonniwell, I wonder if you would mind telling me just who this Mr. Barat is —the younger one."

"He's a gambler," Bonniwell said. "You remember he was on the train with us."

"I know that," Lou Sager said. "I remember them both, but —he's making an awfully big play for that poor Simmons girl. He seems to know her uncle."

"Everybody knows her uncle. He's known as One Percent Simmons."

Eleanor Simmons came out of the log cabin, talking with Jeff Barat. She did not look in Bonniwell's direction. He nodded to Lou Sager and climbed up to his perch again. The others got on the stage. And then they were off again.

"Four minutes ahead of time," said Billy Coogan. "Maybe I'll set a record this trip."

"You'll set a record if you get us there on time," Tom Waggoner said dryly.

They were thirty minutes out of the station when Bonniwell first saw the riders. They were more than two miles away and riding parallel with the coach. They kept that distance for another ten minutes and then came closer. Tom Waggoner saw them, then.

"John!" he exclaimed. "Look to the right."

"I've been watching them," said Bonniwell. "There're eight of them."

Billy Coogan cracked his whip over the lead team. The animals were already going as fast as they could.

After a few minutes Bonniwell said, "Pull up, Billy. We might as well have it out with them here and now."

"Are you going to fight them, John?" asked Waggoner.

Bonniwell shrugged. "You don't want to lose your payroll, do you?"

"No."

The riders were within a half mile when the stage pulled up in a cloud of dust.

Jeff Barat tumbled out.

"Are we going to stand them off?" he cried.

Bonniwell did not reply. He picked up the Winchester, took careful aim and squeezed the trigger. The gun made a tremendous roar as the huge bullet went singing out into space. Bonniwell levered another bullet quickly into the chamber, aimed and fired again.

"A horse down!" cried Tom Waggoner. "Man, what shooting!"

The riders were suddenly spreading out, but they were still coming on. A bullet hummed through the air several feet from Bonniwell.

He continued firing until he had sent six bullets at the highwaymen. Then he suddenly began climbing down from his perch.

"Everybody out and down on the ground!" he ordered.

The passengers began climbing out on the side away from the approaching riders. Bonniwell slammed a couple of cartridges into the Winchester, rested the big rifle against the side of the coach, and sent a bullet towards the leading bandit, now less than a quarter of a mile away.

He grunted in satisfaction when he saw the horse break its stride and throw its rider. He fired once more with the rifle, then dropped it and picked up the shotgun he had brought down with him. But it wasn't necessary. The bandits had had enough of Bonniwell's long distance shooting. They suddenly broke and wheeled back the way they had come, two horses carrying double.

"That's all," said Bonniwell.

"They got enough of your shooting!" exclaimed Billy Coogan.

"God, what a country!" exclaimed Ferdinand Barat, picking himself up off the ground.

The girls were getting into the stagecoach again. Lou Sager stopped to flash a smile at Bonniwell. The minister was the last to get in. He stopped with one foot on the step and turned to Bonniwell.

"If they had come all the way, what would you have done?" he asked.

Bonniwell looked him squarely in the eye.

"I would have killed as many as possible," he replied.

The bandits disappeared over the horizon and the stagecoach resumed its journey. About seven o'clock they stopped at a station for supper. Jeff Barat negotiated so that he would sit next to Bonniwell.

"I liked your work yesterday," he said to Bonniwell. "I liked it even better today."

Bonniwell grunted and continued cutting meat.

"I'm going to locate in Broken Lance," Barat continued. "I need some good men. I'd like to have you with me, Bonniwell."

"Doing what?"

"Whatever's necessary. I've got a hunch Broken Lance is going to grow, and I figger on going into the real estate business."

Bonniwell was thoughtful for a moment. Then he said, "Let's talk about it again in Broken Lance. I may not like the town well enough to stay."

This was the last stop they made. They reached the town of Broken Lance at a dead run shortly after ten o'clock. Broken Lance was small. It consisted of a mere huddle of buildings. It wasn't so small, however, that there weren't two saloons in the town. Before he climbed down from his perch, Bonniwell spoke to Waggoner. "You've been here before, Tom. Will you see about finding lodgings for the women folk?"

"Sure. I was going to do it, anyway. There's a Mrs. Kelsey has some rooms."

Bonniwell turned over the rifle and shotgun to the express agent of Broken Lance and clumped up the street to the closest saloon. It was a smaller edition of the roaring saloons of Baker. It was quite well patronized. He went inside and had one glass of whisky to cut the dust from his throat.

Ten minutes later Tom Waggoner came in.

"What do you think of Broken Lance, John?" he asked.

"It doesn't look like much."

"No, but you just wait about five or six days, when folks hear that the railroad's coming in this direction. Then you'll see a stampede like you never saw in your life. This is going to be a permanent city, not like Baker or the others."

"Tom," Bonniwell said, "do you suppose the Barats know?"

"Not unless they got an inside tip somewheres. Even the workmen don't know which way the road goes. Only the chief engineer and some of the boys at the top."

"Ferd Barat was a big man in New York. I read in the papers that he was knee deep in railroads. I figure, Tom, it's got to be something big that would bring him out here to this country. He doesn't like it."

"Broken Lance is going to be big, but I'd hate to see a couple of wolves like those Barats get a strangle hold on this town. John—" he caught hold of Bonniwell's arm suddenly —"let's step aside here a minute."

When they were out of earshot of the other patrons of the saloon, Tom Waggoner spoke in a low, excited tone. "You've got about eight hundred dollars. Counting the money you paid me back I've got about that much myself. There's several people who know me here and will lend me money."

"Why do you want money?" Bonniwell asked.

Waggoner gripped Bonniwell's arm. "I've got a hunch about those Barats and I want to beat them. Look. They figger they've got the inside track, but they're not going to do anything this evening. You and I are. We're going to buy up as much of Broken Lance as we can—tonight. If we don't, the Barats will grab it tomorrow. I've got a survey of Broken Lance in my carpetbag. Let's go take a look at it."

Tom Waggoner was well known in Broken Lance. He had spent a week here, surveying for the railroad. When Waggoner and Bonniwell entered the Broken Lance Saloon and Dance Hall, it was not long before Waggoner was greeted on all sides.

Waggoner picked out a man at a faro layout, waited until he had lost a small bet, then tugged at his sleeve. "Like to talk to you a minute, Mr. Sheidler."

"Why, sure, Mr. Waggoner," Sheidler exclaimed heartily. They moved to one side and Waggoner introduced Bonniwell. "Mr. Sheidler, shake hands with John Bonniwell."

Sheidler's eyes narrowed speculatively. He held out his hand. "I've heard of you, Mr. Bonniwell. Guess everyone around here has. You goin' to stay in Broken Lance?"

"For a while, maybe."

"You own some land here, Mr. Sheidler," Waggoner said quietly. "Wonder if you'd be interested in selling it?"

A pleased expression came to Sheidler's face. "I've got a hundred and sixty acres, right outside of Broken Lance," he said. "If any fool'd offer me two dollars an acre for it, he'd have it so quick he wouldn't know what'd happened."

"The railroad's coming to Broken Lance," said Waggoner. "Your land will go up in value."

Sheidler shrugged. "It's gettin' crowded around here. For three hundred dollars extra I'll throw in the block I own across the street."

"You've made a sale, Mr. Sheidler," declared Waggoner. "I'll pay you fifty dollars right now to bind the bargain and the balance soon's I can get the money out of the company bank."

Waggoner pulled a notebook out of his pocket, scribbled a bill of sale and handed it to Sheidler to sign. As simply as that Sheidler's property changed hands.

They had a drink, then Waggoner pulled Josh Hudkins out of a poker game.

"How's the store, Josh?" he asked amiably.

"Not so good, Tom," replied Hudkins. "If you'd hurry up and bring your railroad to Broken Lance I might do some business in buffalo hides, but the way things are now it costs too much to freight them to Baker. Don't leave no profit."

"The railroad's coming, Josh," Waggoner told the merchant. "Be here in a month."

"By then, I won't be in business. Not the mercantile business anyway. On'y thing worth while around here is the saloon business."

"I'll buy your store, Josh," said Waggoner, "just the building and the vacant lot next to it. I'll give you five hundred dollars for it. It'll help you hang on until the railroad comes."

"It's a deal."

"Fine—and you'll get free rent for six months."

He paid Hudkins fifty dollars down, with which the merchant promptly returned to the poker game. He told the poker players about his good fortune, and that resulted in Bonniwell's buying two town lots and a couple of tracts on the near-by prairie. The sellers promptly went out to spread the good news.

By eleven o'clock in the evening, Waggoner was sitting behind a table conducting a thriving real estate business. Bonniwell sat at his elbow, saying nothing but not missing a thing. The citizens of Broken Lance were lined up to sell property of dubious title to Waggoner. Whatever they received for the land was clear profit, they reckoned. When they had settled on it, it had not belonged to anyone. There was just as free land to be had for the taking a few miles away from Broken Lance.

Waggoner's honesty cost him the purchase of a few pieces, however. He insisted on telling everyone that the railroad was coming to Broken Lance, and some of the wise ones prudently decided to hold their property.

At ten minutes after twelve, the Barat Brothers stormed into the saloon. Jeff Barat's face was dark with ill concealed anger; his brother kept himself better in hand, but his face was stiff.

"Hold everything!" Jeff Barat cried out. "Waggoner's not the only one here who's buying property. I'll pay twice the amount that he's paying for anything in Broken Lance or within five miles. And we're paying all cash!"

The saloon exploded. Someone fired a gun into the floor and a half dozen other citizens of Broken Lance promptly followed his example. Everyone whooped and shouted.

"I guess that finishes us," Tom Waggoner said to Bonniwell.

Bonniwell shrugged. His mind wasn't really on this, at all. He was thinking of the two girls from the East. Eleanor Simmons probably believed that the discharging of the guns meant a killing.

"You own about enough, don't you?" he asked of Tom Waggoner.

Waggoner shrugged. "More than half of the actual real estate of the town as it now is, and about a thousand acres of land near by. But the big acreage hasn't been touched yet. The man who gets Ollie Simmons' ranch will hold the key to Broken Lance."

"Can you buy his place?"

Waggoner laughed shortly. "That depends. If money's required, no. You don't know him, do you?"

"No. But—the girl who came on the stage with us, Eleanor Simmons, she's Ollie's niece. Come to live with him."

Waggoner whistled. "Why'd he ever let her come here? His place's not the sort you'd want to bring a girl to. You know how he got his start?"

"I've heard he's called One Percent."

"Yeah, he got the name by taking a toll of one percent from all the trail herds that passed here. And you know your Texas trail riders, John."

"I know them," said Bonniwell. His mouth twisted briefly. "It's hard to believe that *anyone* could cut their herds."

"Ollie Simmons could. He's got half the thieves and killers in Kansas on his ranch."

Bonniwell wondered what Eleanor Simmons would think when she reached her uncle's ranch, when she learned the truth about him.

"Well, if we're finished for tonight, Tom," he said, "I think I'll get a room and turn in."

"Me, too. We can't compete against the sort of money the Barats are shelling out."

All of Broken Lance, it seemed, was crowded about the Barat brothers. They paused at the edge of the swirling crowd and heard a town lot being sold for five hundred dollars.

"They're going to need a lot of money at the rate they're buying," said Waggoner, as they went out to the little cubbyhole that served as the hotel lobby.

They engaged two rooms on the second floor, mere alcoves with thin planks for walls.

Chapter Six

LAW MAN

BONNIWELL ROSE before nine, which was early for Broken Lance. But oddly, the town was awake and active. He guessed that it hadn't really gone to bed the night before. Across the street in the restaurant, he discovered that his guess was correct.

The Barats were here. They were at a round table, eating

breakfast and at the same time dickering with a couple of roughly dressed men. When Bonniwell got a small table near the window, Jeff Barat left his brother to continue the bargaining and came and sat down opposite Bonniwell.

"Ran a shindy on me, huh, Bonniwell?" he said.

"I don't get you."

"I asked you twice yesterday to throw in with me. You said you'd think it over. All the time you were planning to get the edge on me, with that partner of yours, the damn railroad——"

"Barat!" Bonniwell cut him off. "Tom Waggoner's my best friend."

"What of it?" snapped Jeff Barat. "He's usin' his job with the railroad to clean up here——"

"How did *you* get the informatioin about Broken Lance?" Bonniwell asked quietly. "Did you just *guess* the railroad was coming here?"

"My brother's been interested in railroads for years," said Jeff. "He's been associated with the big men, Vanderbilt, Fisk, Gould——"

"I've read about him in the papers."

Barat put both his hands flat on the table in front of him. "Bonniwell, I'm going to talk turkey to you. My brother and I are going to be the big men around here. There's nothing can stop us. I told you yesterday, I liked your style and I'm saying it again. I can use a man like you. Throw in with me——"

"No," said Bonniwell.

For just a second Barat's face was unguarded and showed his thoughts. Then he got control of it again. He smiled thinly. "Sorry you can't see it that way, Bonniwell. Well, we can be friendly competitors, eh?"

"Not competitors—or friends."

Barat got up. "What are you trying to do, pick a fight with me?"

"Not at all. Only you've been trying to force yourself upon me and I prefer to pick my own friends. That's putting it plainly."

Barat's face got white. His hands, hanging at his sides, clenched and unclenched. Then suddenly he turned and went back to his brother's table.

The waitress came to Bonniwell's table, but before he could give his order Tom Waggoner came in, with Lou Sager on his arm.

Bonniwell stared at Lou Sager. Heretofore he had seen her only in traveling clothes, her face dull from fatigue. Now she was refreshed, bright-eyed and sparkling. And she was wearing a dress that would have attracted attention at the Planters Hotel in St. Louis.

She saw his eyes regarding her. "Like it?"

He nodded. "It's very becoming."

"I made it myself. I make all my clothes."

Waggoner helped her into a chair. That brought him facing the window. He exclaimed. "There's Ollie Simmons!"

Bonniwell frowned slightly. "Do you mind? I want to see someone at the hotel."

He saw the question in Lou Sager's eyes, but bowed and left the restaurant. He walked casually across the street to the Broken Lance Hotel. There were a dozen horses in front of it, also a buckboard, evidently intended for the transportation of Ollie Simmons' niece.

Ollie Simmons and his riders had already gone inside. Bonniwell heard them in the saloon and walked in. Jack McSorley with a glass at his lips saw him and whooped.

"John Bonniwell!"

He grabbed Bonniwell's hand and pumped it. "So they didn't get you, after all. I told them five or six Texas men couldn't do it!" He whirled. "Ollie, this is John Bonniwell!"

Ollie Simmons was as much like a grizzly bear as a human could be. He was six feet four, almost four feet broad at the shoulders and had a fierce black beard that came down to his chest. His hands were enormous. Bonniwell had to steel himself against the tremendous pressure of the handshake.

"Glad to shake your hand, Bonniwell!" boomed Simmons. "Provided you're not figurin' on takin' the job of marshal of Broken Lance."

Jack McSorley, who was only two inches less in height than his employer Simmons, roared at that. "Be too bad for us if he did, huh, Ollie?"

There was a glitter in Ollie Simmons' eyes, and less good humor in his tone when he replied. "It might be a bit o' trouble, at that."

A slight, wiry man edged around from behind Ollie Simmons' huge bulk. He was clean shaven except for a black mustache, and his face bore absolutely no expression. But

Bonniwell got a glimpse of the pale, washed-out blue eyes and brought his gaze back upon them.

"Coe's my name, Russ Coe," the man said. He made no move to shake hands. "I guess you knew a friend o' mine—Pete Vinson."

Bonniwell remembered Vinson. He had drawn against Bonniwell in the early days of Haleyville. He had never met Russ Coe before, but knew of him by reputation and knew that a more cold-blooded man did not live in all of Kansas.

"Yes, I remember Vinson," he replied. "Why?"

Jack McSorley reached out with a big hand and placed it on Russ Coe's chest. "None of that, now, Russ. Bonniwell's a friend of mine."

"Is he?" said Coe, without taking his eyes off Bonniwell.

The Barats, storming into the saloon, broke the tension.

"Ollie Simmons, I want to talk to you," Jeff Barat announced.

Ollie Simmons hunched his huge shoulders.

"Don't know's I want to listen to you, Barat," he rumbled. "I ain't forgotten the last time I talked to you. It was about four aces!"

"I don't remember!" snapped Jeff Barat. "So it couldn't have been important. *This* is. Meet my brother, Ferdinand. He's one of the biggest men in Wall Street. I told him this was a good spot to invest some of his idle capital, so———"

Bonniwell went out. He almost collided with Eleanor Simmons, standing in the little hotel lobby. She was looking into the saloon, as if she didn't quite dare go in.

She was very pale today and Bonniwell was sure that her chin was trembling a little. Her eyes met his and he saw the pain in them. He'd resolved not to intrude himself upon her again, but he couldn't help himself now. "Your uncle know you're here?"

She shook her head and her eyes became suddenly bright with tears. "I—which one is my uncle?"

He turned to look back into the saloon. "The big one with the beard. I'll tell him you're here."

He went back into the saloon and signaled to Ollie Simmons. When he caught his eye he jerked his head toward Eleanor, in the lobby. Simmons saw the girl; in the middle of a violent denunciation of Jeff Barat, he brushed past the gambler.

He went right to Eleanor and wrapped her in a big bear embrace. Bonniwell, on his way out of the hotel, saw Eleanor flinch from her uncle.

He went back to the restaurant across the street. Waggoner and Lou Sager were almost finished with their breakfast.

"I understand you and Tom have become big real estate men overnight," Lou flashed at Bonniwell as he sat down.

"There are a couple of fellows who are bigger," Bonniwell replied. He grinned at Tom Waggoner. "The Barats are trying to give Ollie Simmons the rush act, but Ollie isn't very friendly. He remembers something about four aces that Jeff Barat once pulled on him."

"That's fine!" exclaimed Waggoner. "While I don't consider Ollie Simmons an asset to the country, for the time being I prefer that he remain in *status quo*. He'll act as a sort of buffer between us and the Barats."

Bonniwell was thoughtful. "Barat's got something up his sleeve, Tom. He's a handy man with a gun himself, but he's biting off a pretty big mouthful if he tries to tackle Ollie Simmons by himself. What's this town got in the way of law, Tom?"

"None. The county seat is Baker. One of the first things we've got to do is form a company or town council. I was intending to talk to the business men about that this morning."

"That's my hint to leave," said Lou Sager. She pushed back her chair, but paused. "Tom has just rented me a store. I've got to figure out what fixtures and supplies I'll need." Her eyes were on Bonniwell's face, quite evidently seeking approbation for her venture. But Bonniwell didn't give it to her.

His eyes were slightly narrowed and he grinned in an absent-minded manner. The color rose in Lou Sager's face. She smiled at Tom Waggoner, rose quickly and left the restaurant.

"She's really going to open a millinery store?" Bonniwell asked of Waggoner then.

"Of course. You and I started the land boom last night. By tomorrow the news will be in Baker. You'll see a stampede to Broken Lance. And in a month, when the railroad comes here, this town will be headquarters for the southwest. I'm quitting my job with the railroad."

"Why, Tom?"

Waggoner shrugged. "Won't be able to do justice to it. Besides, anyone can carry on the railroad work from now.

It's been a good job, but I figure a man's got to try to better himself when he gets the opportunity. And this is my opportunity."

"She's a plucky girl," said Bonniwell.

Waggoner grinned. "I've got my eye on her. I'm betting she makes a go of it."

After breakfast Bonniwell went to the hotel and sat down on a chair on the veranda. Tom Waggoner left him to talk to various business men. He came back for Bonniwell shortly after eleven. "Havin' a meeting in Hudkins' store, John. Come along."

Almost a dozen of the town's leading citizens were gathered in Josh Hudkins' store when they got there. They'd already been discussing things.

When Bonniwell came in with Waggoner, Josh Hudkins held up his hands for quiet.

"Mr. Waggoner," he said, "we been talkin' things over and we decided that seein's how you're really makin' Broken Lance, you ought to be the first mayor. What say?"

Tom Waggoner smiled boyishly. "Why, I appreciate the compliment, gentlemen, but for certain reasons I'd rather not be the head of Broken Lance's civic body. I'll be glad, however, to assist in drawing up a charter and a city constitution. I helped with the drafting of the one that Baker's now using. I think—" his eyes ran quickly over the crowd—"Mr. Hudkins would make as fine a mayor as we could get."

There was spirited applause at that suggestion. But before anyone could comment on the selection, the door of the store opened and the two Barats came into the store. They seemed to have an uncanny knack for finding out what was going on. This time bluff Ferdinand Barat took the lead.

"Gentlemen," he said in his rich baritone voice, "I believe you're gathered here to form a town company. I have a suggestion to make. My brother Jeff has been in Kansas for years. He is familiar with civic government in a dozen towns like Broken Lance. Incidentally, he has invested heavily in local real estate and as the man from whom you will expect to obtain the largest share of your taxes with which to run this government he should be reckoned with. I propose Jeff Barat as your choice for mayor."

"Hooray!" one man yelled. John Bonniwell's sharp eyes found the man instantly and made a note of him.

But silence lingered over the others. The crowd needed a

leader. Tom Waggoner was the man. "You heard my own endorsement a moment ago, gentlemen. Very well, you've two candidates now. Why don't you vote on them?"

"All those in favor of Jeff Barat for mayor say 'aye'," John Bonniwell said.

"Hooray!" yelled the solitary support of Jeff Barat.

"Those in favor of Josh Hudkins?"

There was no question about that. Bonniwell was watching the faces of the Barats, saw the anger that swept across them. But still they did not withdraw. Ferdinand Barat, in fact, smiled ingratiatingly.

"No hard feelings," he assured the men in the store.

He passed out cigars. So the least they could do, when they got to it, was to elect Jeff Barat to the city council, which consisted of seven men. The other six were: Mayor Hudkins, Ferd Barat, Tom Waggoner, "Beak" Nelson, Doug Fletcher and Charley Sheidler.

Bert Fowler was appointed secretary of the city company. It was voted to employ a city marshal who would, in turn, hire deputies as they were needed when the town grew. As there were no funds in the city treasury at the moment, every one of the sixteen men present contributed a hundred dollars. That required the election of a city treasurer and Ben Hutton was elected to the post. Hutton was the faro dealer at the Golden Prairie Saloon.

When the meeting broke up, Josh Hudkins detained Waggoner and Bonniwell.

"Mr. Bonniwell," he said, "you know what this town's going to be like in a few days. Another Baker and Haleyville. I know what you did in those towns and I want you as city marshal."

Bonniwell shook his head. "I'm sorry, Mr. Hudkins. I never want to have to use my guns again."

"We've got an early start in this town," Waggoner said. "If we keep it tight, we can retain control of it. I'm in favor of getting a strong law enforcement body. But knowing John's attitude toward such a job, I think we'd better look elsewhere."

"But who'll we get?"

"I don't know," replied Waggoner. "But it should be the best man available for the job. Why not try to get Wild Bill Hickok?"

"He's in Hays City. They're paying him pretty high there.

We couldn't meet it. There was a young fellow here a few months ago, I figure would make a swell marshal. But I don't know where I can locate him. He's a buffalo hunter. Name of Wyatt Earp."

"He's a mighty good man," said John Bonniwell. "If you can persuade him to become a peace officer, you'll have the man you want."

"Isn't Lee Thompson in town?" asked Waggoner. "I thought I saw him in the saloon last night."

Hudkins scowled. "Yes, he's here. In fact, he killed Ike Bailey last week. I dunno. Lee's pretty fancy with a gun for me."

"You need a man who's as tough as the toughest, as fast as the fastest. Sure, Thompson's a killer—but can you get along without a killer here?"

Ollie Simmons, by the simple process of taking them, was the owner of five thousand acres of the finest buffalo grass range in Southern Kansas. He was the only cattle king in Kansas.

He had left Illinois in 1858, after selling a fairly prosperous mercantile business, against the advice of his older and steadier brother.

He headed west. At St. Joe, Missouri, he hired out as an ordinary teamster and drove a six mule team to Santa Fe, New Mexico. There he joined a wagon train bound for San Francisco.

Adventure, more than the lure of gold, kept him in the Golden State for two or three years. He roamed the mining camps and enjoyed himself more than he ever had in his life.

Somehow he drifted up to Oregon, at the time when the Montana gold camps were drawing thousands of men from the Pacific Coast. He was at Virginia City and Alder Gulch when Henry Plummer and his amazingly well organized band of "road agents" were terrorizing the mining camps. Simmons became a member of the vigilantes which eventually hanged Plummer and more than thirty of the road agents.

He clawed a few thousand dollars' worth of dust from the gold canyons, but it wasn't enough to hold him. He sold his claim and traveled overland to St. Joe, Missouri, from which he had started out, several years before.

A glib scoundrel from Michigan talked Simmons into sinking all his money into a wagon train headed for Denver.

The savage guerrilla warfare was at its height along the Missouri-Kansas border. The train took a more northerly and westerly route than ordinarily to avoid the guerrillas, and should have got through safely.

Except that the Michigan man sold them out.

One morning a band of guerrillas rode out of a patch of woods near the camp of the wagon train and calmly took the wagons away from the teamsters. Resistance was useless; there were forty men in the band. The teamsters were lucky to escape with their lives. The Michigan man rode off with the raiders.

That experience decided Ollie Simmons upon his eventual course. He liked this country. For six years he had traveled all over the West and had not liked any section as well as this. He had always been in the other man's territory. He decided to make a territory of his own.

Four of the jobless teamsters threw in their lot with him. They helped Simmons build a small fort here on the prairie. They formed the nucleus of a group that eventually numbered almost fifty. Ollie Simmons had been robbed by Kansans. Very well, he would get back from Kansas what he had lost. By the gun, as it had been taken from him.

He robbed emigrant trains, and called it "toll." He built a stronghold on the prairie and gathered about him the roughest, toughest retainers the country produced. When they stopped a wagon train and said the toll was one percent, the freighters protested only verbally. A few tried it with guns and did not fare so well.

Then the war was over between the states, and a venturing Texas cattle man tried to drive a herd of a thousand Longhorn steers over mountains and desert and plains to Illinois. At the Missouri border, ruffians and thieves stampeded the Texan's herd. When the cattleman came to round them up he could not locate a quarter of the animals. He tried again to cross the border and a frontier sheriff turned him back, with the curt order that Texas cattle could not cross into Missouri. The ruffians on the back trail again stampeded the herd, killed a cowboy and ran off with two hundred more head of cattle.

Discouraged, the Texan retreated with his reduced herd. Ollie Simmons offered to get him through to Missouri. The Texan assented gladly. Simmons' redoubtable force delivered a crushing defeat to the border ruffians. Then they intimidated the sheriff who had previously refused to let the herd into Missouri. The Texan sold the cattle in Joplin, Missouri at a very satisfactory price and then learned to his chagrin that Simmons wanted for his services one-half of the proceeds. The Texan could do nothing else but pay. Counting up, he learned that he had actually collected money for only two hundred of the thousand head of Longhorns with which he had first reached Kansas.

Not that it made much difference. The Texan went to a Joplin gambling house and in a single night lost every cent he had. He was on the verge of blowing out his brains when Ollie Simmons made him a proposition.

He gave the Texan the four thousand dollars he had received as his share of the cattle sale, plus an additional two thousand dollars. He told the cattleman to return to Texas, buy as many steers as he could for the six thousand dollars and bring them to Kansas. He, Ollie Simmons, would see that they got to market from there.

To safeguard his investment, Ollie Simmons sent two of his own men with the Texas cattleman.

It was the best thing Simmons had ever done in his life. Texas steers, at home, had a hide and tallow value of $3.00, and it was a bother to skin the animal and render the carcass to tallow. At an average of $4.00, Simmons' emissary bought 1500 of the best beeves in Texas. He gathered together a crew and brought them to Kansas; from there Simmons took them through hostile territory to Springfield, Missouri, where they brought $22.00 a head.

When Simmons reached his home range he discovered to his amazement that two thousand Texas steers were grazing on his own land. With them were twenty-five Texas cowboys, ready, willing and able to defend the herd.

Simmons had to let them pass. He did, however, elicit from this outfit the information that two or three additional herds were expected to make the overland trip. By the time the next one reached the vicinity of Simmons' stronghold, the border chief had recruited additional fighting men.

Simmons bluntly told the drover that the toll for crossing Simmons' land was five percent of his herd. The drover gave fight. He had a dozen men. After casualties, Simmons offered a truce, at one percent. The drover paid it.

Simmons discovered that if he showed strength the drovers would stand for a one percent tax. More than that, though, they would fight.

This was better than driving the herds yourself, risking your money. Simmons' men ranged the prairies for fifty or sixty miles. A couple of his men were often sufficient to force payment of the toll. A cattle herd moved slowly. Drovers came to know that if they repelled the toll collectors, it would invariably mean the arrival of Simmons' entire fighting force inside of twenty-four hours.

In 1867 Abilene came into existence. Simmons collected from the herds that passed near his ranch and turned northeast. He extracted toll from the drovers who took their steers to Caldwell and Hays City, to Newton and Baker.

He took the toll in cattle. He fattened them on his range, and when he needed money for his crew, he drove a small herd to railhead. Buyers and commission men from Chicago and Kansas City were commoner than bartenders in the trail towns. You could sell a herd in five minutes, and get your money right away.

A settler built a store one day, out on the prairie, figuring to get some business from Texas men before they reached the towns farther north. Simmons didn't mind. He and his men patronized the store. Soon there was a saloon. Then another store. And overnight, Broken Lance.

About this time, he received a letter from his brother in Illinois, telling of the long illness of his daughter, Eleanor, a girl Ollie remembered as a child of seven or eight. Ollie, affluent now and playing with the thought of respectability, wrote his brother to send the girl.

She came, and when he saw her, he knew that it was a mistake. She was unlike the few women he'd known out in this country. Eleanor was decidedly a product of civilization.

But if he was disturbed by Eleanor, the latter was even more disconcerted by Ollie Simmons. Her father was a respected doctor in a quiet Illinois village. He was poor, but he was educated and refined. Whatever refinement her uncle might once have had, had vanished with his years in the West.

There were seven or eight wild looking men in the party that rode out to the Simmons Ranch. A few rode in advance of the buckboard and a few behind. Her uncle rode with her and tried to make conversation.

"Too bad Roland won't come out here. If he did he'd make more money in a year than he'll make in Benton in ten. This country needs a good doctor."

"I don't believe father's interested in money," Eleanor defended her father.

Ollie Simmons snorted. "That's why he's always been so damned poor. Why, I remember when I was in Benton myself. Half his patients never paid him at all, and the other half gave him chickens and hogs and garden truck. I don't think Roland got any hard money in a month."

Her uncle's statement was painfully true. Her father still never sent a patient a bill. He accepted whatever they could pay.

She said to her uncle: "Father's not at all well. I think he ought to visit this country for awhile himself."

"Try and get him to leave that precious Benton," exclaimed Ollie Simmons. "Why, I sent him money last year to come out and stay with me. He sent the money back."

"I remember," Eleanor said quietly.

"He's poor, huh? Well, so was I, ten years ago, Eleanor. Do you know how much I'm worth today?"

"No, I don't, but—a man told me you were one of the wealthiest men in this country."

"He didn't lie. I own twenty thousand head of cattle and five thousand acres of land."

And then they came in sight of the ranch buildings. From a distance they were disappointing. They seemed to be a mere cluster of flimsy shacks, but when they approached Eleanor saw that the main house was built of logs.

A Negress, so fat she could scarcely waddle, was awaiting them in front of the house.

"Ah's Emily," she introduced herself. "An' ah's sho' glad to have a lady comin' to this-yeah house."

The inside of the house, Eleanor discovered, was scrupulously clean, although far too rough and mannish. Chairs were straight-backed. There were no curtains, no pictures on the walls, none of the little touches about a house that a woman liked.

Her uncle showed her about the house and said, "Write down what you think we need, and we'll order it from Kansas City or St. Louis."

Eleanor protested, "But I'm only here on a visit. You don't have to buy a single thing extra for me." Ollie Simmons took her arm gruffly. "You're stayin' here for quite a spell. You can help me by getting this place furnished like it should be. Uh—somethin' like the houses back in Illinois."

"That would cost a lot of money."

"Money?" Ollie Simmons laughed shortly. "I told you I was the richest man in these parts. An' I'm goin' to be richer in a few years. I figure to own a hundred thousand head of cattle some day."

Dinner was served in the kitchen at a plain, uncovered table. Eleanor ate with her uncle and two of the men who had been to town with him, Jack McSorley and Russ Coe.

"The other boys have a special shack for eatin'," her uncle explained.

"They eat with their knives," said Russ Coe.

Ollie Simmons looked sharply at Coe, but the latter kept his eyes down on his plate. Jack McSorley, who had shaved and slicked down his hair since Eleanor had seen him last, sat stiffly at the table. He spoke only when her uncle addressed him. He was the first to leave the table.

After dinner, Ollie Simmons went out to look after some things and Eleanor followed him to the veranda, where she sat down to look over the ranch yard.

She was there when Russ Coe came casually from around the rear of the house.

"A little class is what this place's been needing," he said.

Eleanor had been thinking just before Coe showed up, what attitude she should take toward the men on the ranch. It was a problem that had not occurred to her until she had observed Coe and McSorley at the dinner table.

She looked coolly at Coe. "Class?"

He grinned: "Yeah—somethin' like you."

Eleanor cocked her head to one side. "Mr. Coe, my uncle neglected to tell me. Just what is your position on this ranch?"

Russ Coe's grin faded away. "I'm a sort of foreman."

"Oh, then you're a very busy man. I understand there's an enormous amount of work to be done every day." Eleanor's eyes left Coe's face and looked toward the corrals beyond. It was so blunt and obvious that Coe couldn't help but get it.

He stiffened, muttered something under his breath and clumped away. At one of the bunkhouses, a hundred feet away, he turned and looked back at Eleanor.

58

It wasn't the most tactful thing for Eleanor to do, but she knew Russ Coe was the sort of man she must squelch right at the start, or suffer endless annoyance from him in the days to come.

An hour or so later, Jack McSorley came upon a small group of cowboys, chuckling over some things Russ Coe was telling them. McSorley heard only the tail end of a remark: ". . . a high-toned lady. We're gonna have to remember we're only poor white trash!"

McSorley caught Russ Coe's arm and whirled him around. "That's the last time you'll ever even mention her around here!" he snarled. "Understand that, Coe?"

Coe sneered at the big foreman. He half turned to the cowboys and appealed to them, in ridicule. "Jack's fallen for——"

And then McSorley hit him, a pile-driving blow that smashed Coe back against the bunks. He fell to the floor on his knees. From that position he looked up at McSorley. There was a gun in the foreman's hand.

"I mean it, Coe," said McSorley. "One word and I'll kill you!"

Russ Coe knew it. He made a tremendous effort and forced a smile. "I was only jokin'."

The next morning at breakfast Eleanor timidly produced some sheets of paper. "I've made a list of some things we might get, Uncle Oliver."

"Fine. Take it in to Josh Hudkins in Broken Lance. What he hasn't got he'll order for you."

"How'll I get to town? If I had a riding dress and a side-saddle I could ride."

Her uncle frowned. "Never saw a woman riding a horse around here. If you don't mind, use the buckboard. I'll have Mose drive you."

Mose was Emily's husband. He did odd jobs around the ranch. He was a strapping Negro who had been a slave only a few years ago.

He brought the team of horses and the buckboard around to the house. Then Ollie Simmons came out and spoke to Eleanor.

"Been thinkin' it over. Broken Lance is going to be a tough town from now on. I'll feel better if you have one of the boys ride with you whenever you go in. Russ Coe——"

"Russ Coe's a gun-fighter, isn't he?" Eleanor asked.

Her uncle spread his palms upward. "He's handy with a gun."

"Would you mind—could it be somebody else?"

"Jack sent all the boys out this mornin', but I guess he could go with you himself."

In that way Jack McSorley became Eleanor's escort on her trips to Broken Lance. He rode his horse in the rear of the buckboard. He did not speak to her except when she addressed him.

Eleanor spent two hours with Josh Hudkins. When she was finished, Mose had loaded the buckboard high with things and Eleanor had made further arrangements to have a wagon-load of things delivered to the ranch.

It was noon when she was ready to go home. Knowing that it would take them an hour and a half to reach the ranch, Eleanor gave Mose a half dollar. "Buy yourself some lunch, somewhere," she told the Negro.

His grin reached to both ears. "Yas-sum, Miss Simmons, thank yuh!" He whirled and rushed across the street to a door over which was a sign, "Saloon."

On her way to the restaurant where she had eaten breakfast the day before Eleanor passed a small store and caught sight of a bright colored gingham dress swirling about inside. She looked a second time and recognized Lou Sager, a bandanna handkerchief about her head, busy with a broom.

She went in.

"So you're really going to start a store?" she commented, smilingly.

"My order's already in St. Louis," Lou Sager replied. "I expect to be open for business inside of a week. And you—how'd you find the ranch?"

"It's enormous. I've been buying some things for the house. I think I'm going to like it out here."

"So'm I. Tom—Mr. Waggoner, whom you know, says this is going to be one of the most important towns in the state. He expects a tremendous boom. You'll notice that the population has already doubled in two days. Where they came from no one knows. Mr. Waggoner bought some of the property around here and then the Barats began outbidding him on everything."

Eleanor couldn't help but note the constant references to "Mr. Waggoner" and "Tom." She smiled. "Will you have lunch with me, Miss Sager?"

"I will—if you won't call me Miss Sager. My name's Lou."

"And mine's Eleanor!"

They were scarcely seated in the restaurant than Tom Waggoner came in. He greeted them with his usual enthusiasm. "I saw you come in. I left several prospective land-buyers to join you."

"Oh, but you shouldn't have!" exclaimed Eleanor.

He grinned. "It's all right. I'm not selling land. I'm buying."

Jeff Barat coming into the restaurant at that moment heard the last of Waggoner's remark.

"You've bought too much land, Mr. Waggoner," he said. "You've beat me out on some choice parcels."

"Do you mind very much?"

Jeff Barat smiled pleasantly. "No, not much. All right if I join you and the ladies at lunch?"

"Of course," said Eleanor. Lou Sager smiled, a bit thinly. Waggoner wasn't any too cordial to Jeff Barat, but the gambler did not mind. He was fully capable of carrying the conversation all by himself, and he did. Eleanor got practically no chance to talk to Lou Sager, whom she wanted to know more intimately.

Later, when she was climbing into the wagon and Mose was turning the team, she saw John Bonniwell walking by on the sidewalk. He nodded to her and tipped his hat. She flashed him a tardy smile. And thought about him, then, half the way to the ranch.

Chapter Seven

BOOM TOWN

ONE DAY BROKEN LANCE was a sleepy hamlet along the Chisholm Trail, the next it was a roaring boom town. The hundred yard Main Street stretched out to a half mile, and four cross streets were cut into the town. From morning to late at night the streets were a mass of moving wagons, men, horses and mules.

Stages came in twice a day from Baker. But freight wagons,

covered wagons came in every hour. And in between, men on horses and mules raced one another, to be the first to get what was coming to Broken Lance.

Tent stores popped up everywhere. Everywhere hammers rang and saws buzzed. Claptrap buildings went up. Where the lumber came from no one seemed to know.

But suddenly it was there, a regular lumber yard and busy twenty-four hours of the day.

Tom Waggoner opened an office in the lobby of the Golden Prairie saloon. Two days later he moved to a building that had just gone up across the street. Somewhere he found a man who could do clerical work and employed him. Then he was able to spend his time outside. All the tent stores that went up, all the false fronted frame shacks, owed their existence to Tom Waggoner.

He did not sell a single town lot, but he leased them. It was a strange way of doing business, but the newcomers agreed to everything.

No one questioned the legality of the election that had made Josh Hudkins mayor of Broken Lance. Everyone was too busy making money and spending it.

The mayor thought it over a day and then employed Lee Thompson as marshal of the town. Thompson was a cold-eyed, lean man of about twenty-five. He had a reputation that was known in three states. Before the end of the week he employed Joe Boots, a half-breed buffalo skinner, as deputy marshal.

Lou Sager's store was ready in three days. Three days later her merchandise came; a couple of hundred ready made hats, materials for making more. When she had come to Broken Lance there had been two in the town. At the end of the first week there were two hundred.

They came with the saloons, of which there were now sixteen. A doctor arrived in town the second week and found plenty of work.

Bonniwell watched Broken Lance grow up around him and he didn't like it. When Waggoner moved to the building across the street from the Golden Prairie Saloon he moved with him. There was a partition at the back of the store, behind which they set up cots. But there was no window in back and it was too gloomy to remain out of sight all day. So Bonniwell was compelled to spend much of his time either in the front office or out on the street. He preferred the street.

He was the only drone in Broken Lance. Everyone else seemed to have plenty to do. So he saw Broken Lance develop. He got to know by sight almost every newcomer to the city. He saw every building go up and he became a little quieter every day, if that were possible.

Jeff Barat bought the Broken Lance Saloon and Dance Hall. It developed that he already owned the two buildings next door. He tore out the walls between, patched up the front and made of the three stores the largest building in town. And almost all of the first floor he converted into a saloon and dance hall. Sections were added to the bar until it was seventy-five feet long, running along the entire rear of the big building. Jeff publicly threw away the key to the front door.

"This place is open twenty-four hours a day!" he declared.

He divided his time between the saloon and his brother's office in the Barat building across the street. This was a new building, a rather solidly constructed one, but built with tremendous speed. Ferd Barat seldom left it once he moved in. Bonniwell, passing every day, saw new desks installed regularly, new employees added. He saw the sign hung out which read "Barat Brothers Bank of Broken Lance. Real Estate. Loans."

A man put a chair outside the bank and sat there from morning until late at night. He was a squat, swarthy individual of about thirty. His name was Mike Slingerland. When Ferd Barat came briefly out of the bank to get his meals, Slingerland left his chair and followed the banker.

Bonniwell gambled moderately. Usually he patronized the Golden Prairie Saloon, but when the huge new place of Jeff Barat was opened for business he went there to see what it was like. He had a drink at the bar, wandered idly around. Bonniwell noted at least a dozen men in the throng who did not play, who stood near each game with hands near their guns. One was seated openly on a raised platform overlooking the faro layout, which normally received the biggest play.

Even before his brother had a bodyguard, Jeff Barat acquired a shadow, a gun-fighter named Kelso, who had an unsavory reputation.

Bonniwell believed him to be a horse thief and highwayman.

And then a train of wagons accompanied by two hundred wild Irishmen came to Broken Lance. It was the advance guard of the railroad. From then on Broken Lance was never the same. A railroad station sprang up in a single day, loading pens the next. A few days later Broken Lance citizens began riding out to watch the grading and the laying of the track.

Day by day the railroad came closer to Broken Lance. Before it reached the town, there was an impediment—a sea of bawling Longhorn cattle. The Texas trail drivers who usually drove their cattle a hundred miles farther, decided that the short buffalo grass surrounding Broken Lance was excellent beef fodder. They decided they'd be better off financially by fattening their stock for a month at Broken Lance, than driving farther and shipping sooner.

That was when the trouble began. The cattlemen knew of One Percent Simmons. They went miles out of their way to avoid crossing the acres he claimed. But now there was a city near Simmon's ranch, and a railroad shipping yard.

There were three thousand Longhorns in the first Texas herd to reach Broken Lance. Accompanying the herd were twenty hard-bitten riders. They had avoided One Percent Simmons' Ranch and were careless. They received a rude shock that evening when fifty men rode down to their camp and surrounded them.

Jeff Barat opened the parley. "You're on my ranch, folks."

The trail boss, a fiery Texas man, snarled at Barat, "What the hell you mean—your ranch?"

"I own all the land hereabouts that isn't owned by Oliver Simmons," replied Barat, grinning hugely. "You been payin' Ollie one percent for the privilege of *crossing* his ranch. But I wouldn't do a thing like that to you. I'll let you graze your herd here for thirty days, until the railroad comes here."

The Texas man saw the fifty armed men, knew that his own group didn't stand a chance. He said: "We'll drive on to Baker."

Barat shrugged. "Suit yourself about that. But—your steers have already trespassed on my land. They've eaten a lot of valuable grass that I needed for my own herd. So you'll have to pay. Two steers in every——"

The Texas man went for his guns. Jeff Barat shot him through the face. Another trail rider tried to avenge his foreman. Kelso, Barat's lieutenant, shot him in the stomach;

then, when he was writhing on his knees, he rode down and coolly sent a bullet through his head.

After that the herd was cut, and if the Barat men took a few more than sixty head, nothing was said. Having paid the tax, the Texas men naturally remained at Broken Lance. They went to the city and talked about their grievance. They drank and they grew resentful. They quarrelled with barkeepers. Lee Thompson buffaloed two of them with his long-barreled six-shooter. He and his deputy threw four more into jail and kept them overnight.

And then, overnight, there were a quarter million Texas Longhorns on the plains surrounding Broken Lance. Two thousand Texas men, each with a year's wages in his pockets, took possession of the town. They outnumbered any other group of residents and they took Broken Lance for their own.

They drank and they fought and they gambled. They rode their horses at breakneck speed up and down the streets of Broken Lance. They shot their guns in the air, now and then sending a bullet through a window.

Broken Lance was Abilene, Newton, Baker, all over again. All rolled into one.

It was hell.

The amazing growth of Broken Lance disconcerted Jeff Barat.

"I've seen other boom towns spring up," he told his brother, "but never one like this."

"The location of this one is ideal," responded his brother, "but what about this cattle business?"

Jeff scowled. "It's about that I wanted to talk. I'm licked. You can hold up a single herd and make the drover give you two percent, but you can't hold up fifty herds, not if they all come in the same week. We've gotten five hundred head of cattle and that's all. If I tried to cut a herd now the Texas men would get together and wipe out Broken Lance."

The older of the brothers frowned. "You told me this man Simmons has been doing it for years."

"He has. But you must remember he was out here alone on the prairie. There weren't as many herds coming through then, and they didn't *all* come this one way."

"I don't like it, Jeff," said Ferdinand. "You assured me we could get fifty thousand head in a year or two. That was the basis of our campaign."

"It doesn't have to be," declared Jeff. "I can squeeze a million dollars right out of Broken Lance in a year."

"Can you?" Ferdinand squinted at his brother. "I never dreamed even a Western town could be as lawless and wild as this one seems to be. How much longer can you keep it under control?"

"As long as I want," retorted Jeff. "I've got some good boys lined up. They keep the cowboys from Texas stirred up, and the peace marshal has his hands so full with them he can't take time to see other things."

"But what about this man Bonniwell? I've heard some things about him."

Jeff shook his head. "Something's wrong with the man. My hunch is he's lost his nerve."

"That feat of his in Baker didn't look like it."

"A flash in the pan. He got all shot up in Haleyville last year, and it's my idea he don't like shooting any more. At any rate, he had the chance to be marshal here and didn't take it."

"He's pretty close with this Waggoner."

"They're old friends. I heard that he don't get any cut from Waggoner."

"He's a fool if he doesn't. Waggoner's making money. He's selling farms, now, to the settlers that are coming in."

"They're suckers. This land isn't any good for farming."

"Perhaps it isn't," said Ferdinand Barat. "But they seem to think it is. I understand Waggoner sold forty acres of land yesterday to a sucker, as you call him, for sixty dollars an acre."

"What? Why he didn't pay over two dollars an acre for the stuff. Say——"

Ferdinand Barat grinned. "I'm ahead of you. We've got a couple thousand acres ourselves. We can get some more, a little ways out. If the boom lasts we won't miss those fifty thousand head of steers you promised me."

The boom not only lasted, but it swelled. When the railroad was two weeks old, it came into Broken Lance twice a day. Each time it disgorged a record load of passengers. And they still came in—on horseback, in covered wagons and even on foot.

Broken Lance had eighteen saloons in its three-block business section. There were two women's clothing shops, now, in addition to Lou Sager's millinery shop. There were three barber shops, two poolrooms and a bowling alley. A man by the name of Bee came in and opened a photographer's establishment. He did a rushing business.

A cowboy came in from the trail. He first got a haircut, then some fancy clothes. After which it was only natural for him to step around to Bee's and get his photograph taken.

A man from New York stopped off one day and rented a large store. From then on Broken Lance had theatrical entertainment. Some of the leading traveling companies of the profession played in Broken Lance. At two dollars admission, the theatre was packed every evening.

Before three herds of Texas Longhorns had reached Broken Lance, a half dozen well-dressed, well-fed men entered the town. They were cattle buyers. They flashed enormous rolls of greenbacks and were very liberal about "setting them up" in the saloons. By the time the first train came to Broken Lance there were fifty cattle buyers, more or less, always in the town.

All the buffalo hunters of the frontier made Broken Lance their headquarters. Josh Hudkins had in his yards, at one time, forty thousand hides. And he shipped twice a week.

With the advent of the farmer and the settler, a new industry sprang up, the buffalo bone business. For ten years the buffalo hunter had been slaughtering the buffalo on the prairies; for countless generations before him, the Indian. The plains were literally covered with bones.

Sven Turnboom bought a forty-acre farm from Tom Waggoner, at forty dollars an acre. He had seven children and a stout wife. The first month he was on his farm, he brought in enough wagon loads of buffalo bones to pay for his entire farm.

It got to be a joke around Broken Lance, that buffalo bones were legal tender.

The buffalo hunters were salty men. There was a natural enmity between them and the Texas cowboys, for the majority of the buffalo hunters were Northerners and had fought in the Union Armies. They were, however, greatly outnumbered by the cowboys, which did not deter them from fighting.

Lee Thompson, the marshal, favored the buffalo hunters. Which didn't go at all well with the cowboys, who maintained that if it weren't for them Broken Lance would roll over and die, and they should therefore be accorded special privileges.

It was Sheidler, the owner of the Golden Prairie Saloon, who instigated the Sunday shooting matches. A mile south of Broken Lance was a small patch of cottonwoods. There was a five-foot swale in front of them and the double protection made an excellent target range.

Sheidler hauled out a couple of barrels of beer, a keg of whisky and opened shop at the tail of a wagon. Every Texas man was a marksman, and the buffalo hunters lived by their skill with guns. They wagered furiously, and shot it out at targets. Which was better than shooting at each other.

The Sunday shooting match got to be an important event. Most of Broken Lance turned out for the occasion, as did every cowboy in miles around.

The second Sunday a couple of Mexican cowboys brought a crateful of vicious fighting roosters. Broken Lance went wild over the sport.

Inside of two weeks, Harrison, the Wells Fargo agent, was complaining about the large number of chicken crates that were coming in to Broken Lance. Certain citizens were sending all over the country for game birds of all sorts and descriptions.

John Bonniwell went out to the shooting matches, but took no part in them, even though he was challenged repeatedly. He was a legend, and men who were themselves expert with guns wanted to see his marksmanship.

Wild Bill Hickok came to Broken Lance one day and stayed over for the Sunday shooting. A group of local sportsmen made up a purse of a hundred dollars to persuade him to give a demonstration.

Hickok consented and amazed the gunhawks with an astounding exhibition of skill. He shot with Frontier Model .44's at a distance of three and four hundred yards and hit a six-inch target. He split a bullet on the edge of a silver dime, cut spots out of playing cards; tying back the trigger of his gun, he demonstrated the art of "fanning" a gun, by striking back the hammer of the pistol with the flattened palm of his hand. The five shots that rolled from the gun sounded almost like one.

Bonniwell, watching, saw however, that Hickok's marksmanship was not very accurate when he fanned the gun. He talked to Hickok later.

"How is it you're not the marshal of Broken Lance, Mr. Bonniwell?" Hickok asked.

He was a tall man with hair that came down to his shoulders. He was the acme of courtesy and had the softest and smallest hands Bonniwell had ever seen on a man of his size.

"Since Haleyville I don't have the hankering for that sort of work," Bonniwell replied.

Hickok nodded. "I've lost it myself. It's bad for the nerves. There wasn't a minute of the time I was in Abilene or Hays that I wasn't expecting a bullet in the back. I'm going to do a bit of scouting for the soldiers. The Sioux will be a relief after these cowboys."

The following Sunday, Bonniwell was drinking a glass of beer at Sheidler's wagon, when he saw most of the crowd moving toward a group of men who were shooting with revolvers at a distance of a hundred yards.

"Kelso and Slingerland are shootin' against a couple of strangers," said a passerby. "They're gettin' beat, too!"

Bonniwell finished his beer and walked over to see the shooting. He came just too late to see the strangers shoot, but Len Kelso was popping away at a paper target, taking careful aim before each shot.

A man who stood near the trees, to one side of the targets, brought up the piece of paper at which Kelso had shot. Kelso looked at it and swore.

"I guess you're beat, pardner!"

The broad-shouldered stake-holder stepped aside to give the money to the conquerors of the Broken Lance pistolmen.

Then Bonniwell saw the two strangers. He drew a soft breath.

One of them was of medium height, smooth shaven, except for a full mustache. The other man was taller and more robust. His face was covered with a short sandy beard. His eyes were slightly staring and he moved as if his muscles were steel springs.

"Anybody else want to shoot?" he asked in a voice that was tense, even though he tried to make it casual.

"For how much?" asked Bonniwell.

The tall man turned a little and saw Bonniwell. He hesitated just an instant before he replied. "Five hundred or a thousand."

"That's pretty steep for me," Bonniwell said, accenting slightly the word "me." "But if you'd care to shoot for just the sport and twenty dollars, say, I'd be glad to accommodate you."

"I'll take you up on that, Mr.——?"

"Bonniwell."

The tall man extended his hand. "My name's Howard. And this is my friend, Mr. Woodson."

Bonniwell shook hands with both "Mr. Woodson" and "Mr. Howard." He had never seen Mr. Woodson before, but he was positive that Mr. Howard was a man he'd encountered on at least two occasions.

"How shall we shoot, Mr. Bonniwell?" asked the man who had given his name as Howard.

"I like a long distance," said Bonniwell.

The man called Woodson suddenly grinned. Howard stiffened, however.

"How about a hundred and fifty yards?" he asked.

"That would be fine. Ten shots apiece? All three of us?"

"No, I'll just watch," said Woodson quickly.

The additional distance was paced off and targets put up.

"Will you shoot first, Mr. Howard?" asked Bonniwell.

Howard shrugged. "Doesn't make any difference." He drew two revolvers from his holsters. Bonniwell noted that one was an old fashioned Navy pistol, the other a Frontier Model .44.

Howard stepped up to the line, threw up one gun and began shooting. He scarcely aimed, and fired the first five shots in less than three seconds. Then he shifted guns and emptied the second gun just as quickly.

He began reloading instantly and was finished when a man brought the target. A murmur of awe ran through the crowd. It was a long range for accurate shooting and the stranger had fired without apparent aim. Yet he had scored seven bull's eyes, and three shots within the circle just outside the bull.

"That's very good shooting, Mr. Howard," said Bonniwell. "It looks as if you'll collect the money."

"I've heard you shoot very well yourself, Mr. Bonniwell," said Woodson, who stood directly behind Bonniwell, a fact of which the latter had not been unaware.

Bonniwell shrugged. He waited until the range was clear, then drew his guns. He smiled at the tall Howard, then turned toward the target and fired. His aiming was as casual as Howard's had been, but if anything the shots came a little quicker. His shift to the left hand gun was a split second faster.

When the man brought the paper target Bonniwell waved it to Mr. Howard. The tall gunman stared at it and wet his lips. "Nine bulls and the tenth just cutting the edge."

The audience, largely Broken Lance citizens, cheered roundly. Some of the Texas men even joined.

"Will you have a glass of beer with us, Mr. Bonniwell?" asked Howard, after he had given Bonniwell two ten dollar gold pieces.

"With pleasure."

But half of the shooters followed them to the refreshment wagon. Bonniwell got beers for himself and the two strangers. The shorter of the two then signaled Bonniwell to come to one side.

When they were out of earshot of others, the taller man asked:

"You know who I am?"

Bonniwell nodded. "We met on a train a few weeks ago. Your brother wasn't with you then."

"How do you know I'm his brother?" asked the man called Woodson.

"There's a family resemblance."

The shorter of the two looked a little worried. Howard said gruffly. "What are you going to do?"

Bonniwell shrugged. "I'm a private citizen. But there are a couple of men in Broken Lance who hail from Jackson County, Missouri."

"We're leaving right away," said the man who called himself Woodson. "We shouldn't have come, but Jess wanted to shoot. How much did you lose on the train, Mr. Bonniwell?"

"About a thousand dollars."

"We won that much today. Give him the money, Jess."

Mr. Howard, whose real name was Jesse James, scowled at his brother. But he produced a handful of money and handed it to Bonniwell.

A minute later the two men were mounting their horses, beautiful black animals. Bonniwell never saw them again. But he heard much of them, from time to time.

Chapter Eight

UNSEEN FOES

TOM WAGGONER said to Bonniwell, "The Texas men have practically taken over Broken Lance."

"They've taken over every town they ever visited," said Bonniwell. "They took Haleyville and Baker, Caldwell and Wichita. They used to tell me the Texas man was a desirable citizen. I've never had occasion to think so. If there are any good Texas men they stay at home."

Waggoner scratched his jaw thoughtfully.

"I've seen their rowdiness elsewhere, of course. I blamed the Kansas men for it. They wanted the drovers to bring their herds to their towns; did everything they could to antagonize them. They cheated them, mistreated and insulted them."

"What do you think Broken Lance is doing to the Texas men? Jeff Barat is charging them two beefs of every hundred for grazing privilege. He gets them into his saloons and takes away their money with his crooked games——"

"What do you mean saloons, John?" asked Waggoner.

"Besides the Broken Lance Saloon, the Barats own The Two Spot, The Texan's Friend, The Last Chance and The Trail's End."

"Are you sure?"

Bonniwell shrugged. "Whether you like it or not, Tom, Jeff and Fred Barat own Broken Lance."

Tom Waggoner cursed softly. "That was the one thing I didn't want to happen. That's why I rented our lots and stores, instead of selling them. I didn't want them to get into the wrong hands."

"You didn't buy enough of Broken Lance," said Bonniwell. "Furthermore, that newspaper that's starting up this week, *The Broken Lance Point*—well, that belongs to the Barats, too."

"That I knew. But he won't make any money from it."

"No? Perhaps not directly. But I know what a newspaper

can do to the community. We had one in Haleyville that was owned by the wrong side."

Bonniwell's prediction was startlingly true. The first issue of *The Broken Lance Point* came out two days later. On the first page was set forth the editor's platform. It read:

BROKEN LANCE IS ROTTEN!

"*The Broken Lance Point* makes its bow to Broken Lance. It is the only time it will bow to Broken Lance. Its policy will be to thrust. It is independent and will remain so. When we decided to establish this newspaper we looked over the situation and decided that of all places in Kansas we knew, none was more suited for our endeavors than Broken Lance. None was more rotten and none needed cleaning up more.

"It is the duty of a newspaper to fight for the community's best interest and it shall be the object of this newspaper always to thrust where a thrust is needed, dig where digging is necessary. The goal toward which we aim is the betterment of Broken Lance. To that end we pledge ourselves.

"The lifeblood of Broken Lance is the cattle trade. Without it, Broken Lance would shrivel up and die. It is the duty of Broken Lance, therefore, to treat the men from our great sister state of Texas as we would want them to treat us, did we go to them with our largess. In the brief time we have been in Broken Lance we have observed things that have shocked us, that have opened our eyes to the crying need for a torchbearer like *The Broken Lance Point*. We have seen Texas men robbed, cheated, swindled, insulted. We marvel that they have not left us in disgust.

"We are rechecking some of the information we have probed, and we intend in our next issue to give the name to specific things that have been done in Broken Lance, to point the lance at individuals who have made Broken Lance what it is—ROTTEN!"

J. A. Monroe, Editor.

The first issue of *The Broken Lance Point* was a complete sellout. The Texas cattlemen bought the paper in batches, took them to their camps and howled and roared.

Tom Waggoner, white with anger, came to John Bonniwell with a copy of the paper. "You said Barat owned this sheet. If he does, this man Monroe's crazy. He's come out against the very things Barat is responsible for."

Bonniwell inclined his head. "Barat's smarter than I gave him credit for, and a hell of a lot more vicious. The Texas men will be out of hand now, and when the next issue comes out and it calls by name certain men reputed to be cheating Texans, and those men are Barat's competitors——"

Waggoner gasped. "Lord. They'd tear this town apart."

"They'll forget about Barat robbing them of a few head of cattle. They'll go after the men mentioned in the paper, and you can be sure Barat won't be one of them."

An hour later three merchants with folded copies of *The Brokn Lance Point* went to call on the editor. They found him ensconced in a little shack next to the Broken Lance Saloon & Dance Hall, a huge cigar in his teeth, boots on a desk.

Inside the door sprawled a couple of men who were often seen in the saloon next door.

"Howdy, gents!" the editor of *The Broken Lance Point* greeted his callers. "Come to put an ad in *The Point*, have you?"

"We have not," said Josh Hudkins, the spokesman of the trio. "We've come to make a protest about this editorial."

Mr. Monroe took his feet off the desk. He was a flabby man of about forty, with an incredibly red nose and the worst teeth that had been seen in Broken Lance.

"Well, well," he said. "So *The Point* stuck you gents. Well, well. You're Mr. Hudkins, the honorable mayor, huh? Hmm, I got a little piece here I was figurin' on printin' in the next issue of *The Point*. It tells how you and a few of the boys pulled a fast election on Broken Lance——"

"You print that and it's the last thing you'll print in this town," Josh Hudkins said ominously.

"Threatening the editor, Mr. Mayor?" chuckled Monroe. "Well, well. I'll have to make a note of that, too. Might make a story for the paper. What else did you have on your mind?"

"Nothin', I guess," said Dog Martin, the cattle shipper. "Nothin' that you'd understand. You're determined to get the Texas men to tear this town apart, and so there ain't no use talkin' to you. The only language you'd understand is——"

He made a quick movement and a Frontier Model Colt with a twelve-inch barrel appeared suddenly in his hand. But he didn't fire it. A voice behind him drawled.

"Drop it, Mister!"

The three visitors had foolishly ignored the two men sitting inside the door. When they turned now, they saw guns in their hands. And somehow they knew that these men wouldn't mind using them.

Dog Martin dropped his gun to the floor. Without a word the three men went out. The editor of *The Broken Lance Point* yelled after them: "That will make a story, too."

An hour later Len Kelso killed a Texas man on the sidewalk before Josh Hudkins' Mercantile Store. The cattlemen, more than slightly drunk, had come out of the store and collided with Kelso.

Kelso disappeared after killing the Texan. But ten minutes later a mob of a hundred cowboys marched down to Josh Hudkins' store and riddled it with bullets. A customer inside was badly wounded. Hudkins escaped injury by dropping to the floor at the first volley.

Bonniwell saw the advancing mob from the entrance of Tom Waggoner's office. When the citizens of Broken Lance took to the stores and buildings, Bonniwell turned casually and went through the office to the back room, where he dropped on a cot.

Tom Waggoner found him there a little while later. "Did you hear the riot?"

"Couldn't help hearing," Bonniwell replied shortly.

"The Texas mob blasted the hell out of Hudkins' store," exclaimed Waggoner. "And it was Kelso who killed that man Hubbard."

"Thompson arrest Kelso?"

"No, he can't find him. I think it's just as well. The Texas men have gone completely wild. Hear that noise?"

"I hear it," said Bonniwell, "and I don't like it. I'm thinkin' of taking a little trip. One'd do you good, too, Tom. You been working pretty hard."

"You mean you think I ought to run out?" exclaimed Waggoner. "Why, I couldn't run now, John. Not until things are settled."

"They won't be settled, Tom. Not for quite a spell. Texas has got Broken Lance treed, and there's nothing you or anyone can do about it. You wanted the Texas cattle trade for Broken Lance and you've got it!"

"Yes, but we didn't bargain for this violence. It wouldn't have happened, either, if Jeff Barat hadn't turned robber, if he hadn't got that damn newspaper——"

"Barat don't give a damn for the Texas business. Not after this year anyway. He figures on making a big enough stake this year so he won't need Texas. The way he's goin' he'll do it, too."

"No, he won't. The Texas drovers need us as badly as we need them. If we treat their men right they'll cooperate with us. We're going to hire a couple more deputy marshals."

Bonniwell took the street an hour later. The Texans had gone to the saloons and were drinking themselves soggy drunk. So unless they were unduly annoyed in the interim they could be expected to remain reasonably quiet for a couple of hours.

He passed Lou Sager's shop, and she saw him through the window and signaled to him. He went inside. She was waiting on a customer, a girl from one of the honky-tonks, and motioned to him to wait. He listened to the conversation.

"I like this hat," the girl from the honky-tonk was saying. "I ain't complainin' about the price, neither. I'll give you twenty dollars instead of fifteen if you'll promise not to sell one just like it to any of the other girls."

"I can promise you that easy enough, Gussie," Lou Sager replied smilingly. "I never sell the same style twice. I'm a woman, too, you know."

"Yeah, sure," agreed the girl called Gussie.

"And the price of the hat is still fifteen dollars," Lou went on. She wrapped it in tissue paper and put it in a square box. "Here you are, Gussie."

Gussie took her purchase, winked at Bonniwell and went out.

"Selling many hats to Texas?" Bonniwell asked then.

A slight frown creased Lou Sager's forehead. "Strangely, no. The Texas men spend all their money before they think of going home. But business is good. That hat I just sold wouldn't have brought more than three dollars in Springfield, Illinois."

"So you like Broken Lance? Isn't it—kind of nerve wracking?"

Lou shuddered. "I hear shooting in my sleep."

"Why don't you go back to Illinois? You can sell out your store at a profit?"

She looked out of the window. "It's pretty hard to go back, John. Isn't it?"

"I've no place to go."

"Where'd you live before you came out here?"

"Indiana. But that was before the war."

She changed the subject. "Have you seen Eleanor Simmons lately?"

Bonniwell was silent for a second, then he said, casually: "The girl who came out here same time we did?"

But he wasn't deceiving Lou Sager. He looked suddenly at her and caught her regarding him with narrowed eyes. He turned to stare out at the street.

"She was in Broken Lance last week," Lou said quietly. "She asked about you."

"How does she like it at her uncle's?"

"I guess you know the answer to that, John. How *could* she like it there?"

"And she can't go home. She's out here for her health."

"Well, she was looking better." Lou Sager drew a deep breath. "Oh, I forgot to mention that she's coming to town again today. In fact, she's coming in right now."

Bonniwell was startled. He had time only to give Lou Sager a reproachful look before Eleanor Simmons came into the millinery shop. She stopped just within the door, and said, "Hello, Lou," and then after a momentary pause, "How do you do, Mr. Bonniwell."

She wore a rather short, fringed skirt, a tan blouse with a bright scarf about her throat, soft elkskin boots. Her blond hair was coiled on the nape of her neck and she wore a cream colored Stetson over it.

She was amazingly attractive in the Western costume—even more beautiful, Bonniwell thought, than she had been in St. Louis that day he had said good-by to her.

He said now: "How do you do. Kansas seems to agree with you."

"Thank you. Broken Lance seems to double in size every week."

She was coolly casual, but disposed to talk to him, anyway.

"In October," he said, "the town will shrivel up. Until spring, anyway."

A faint smile broke her calm voice. "Does it get very cold here in winter?"

"Quite," he began, and then stopped. The door behind Eleanor opened and Jeff Barat came in. He swept off his hat.

"I saw you come in here, Eleanor," Barat said. He shot a triumphant glance at Bonniwell. "You're having dinner with me tonight."

"Hello, Jeff," Eleanor Simmons said. "I don't believe I can stay in town for dinner."

Bonniwell moved to the door. "Got to see someone," he mumbled.

Jeff Barat pretended to see Bonniwell for the first time. "Uh, hello, Bonniwell."

Bonniwell did not look at Eleanor. But Lou Sager moved forward and his glance went involuntarily to her. He caught the expression of pity in her eyes and his lips became tight. He went out and walked stiffly up the street.

To Waggoner's office, less than ten minutes later, came a burly man in a broadcloth suit and a stiff-brimmed black hat.

"Bonniwell!" he exclaimed. "Been lookin' all over town for you."

Bonniwell got up and shook hands. "Jim Westgard! What are you doing in Broken Lance?"

"Business, John. You know I was appointed U. S. Marshal a few months ago?"

"I heard about it, Jim. I figured they picked a good man."

"I don't know. I've got a pretty big district. And our criminal average is kind of high."

"Who're you after? Jesse?"

Westgard sighed. "No, thank the Lord! He's Bob Paulson's worry. My territory is south of the Missouri."

"Jesse was south a few weeks ago——"

"I don't want to hear about it!" Westgard exclaimed quickly. "He held up the state fair at Kansas City only last week. The boys believe he lit out for Missouri and that's good enough for me. I've got my own worry. A big one. Doug Sutherland——"

"What'd he do?"

"He held up a crossroads store over at Bellview. He killed the man who ran it, Jud Stanton, and got $22.00."

"Don't hardly seem like it was worth it."

"No. But Jud Stanton was the postmaster at Bellview and the $22.00 was government money. That makes it my job.

"Doug's usual gang was with him—Rafael Gallegos, Mort Reisinger, Jack Schiffkarten. They must have passed through Broken Lance yesterday or the day before. They know I'm after them."

"I didn't see them. I wouldn't know Doug, anyway."

"About your build, John. Sandy hair and usually a short beard. He's poison. I figure he's headin' for the Indian Nations."

"They usually do. They're hard to get there. The Comanches may take care of him for you."

"I can't depend on them. This Jud Stanton has a cousin who's somebody or other. He's making a big holler. That's why I stopped in to see you."

"Me, Jim?"

"Yes, I can guarantee you ten dollars a day and mileage to go after Doug. You know that country as well as any man south of the Missouri. I can't spend any more time going after him myself and I've got to get someone. I figure you're the best man for the job."

John Bonniwell frowned. "I didn't intend to wear a badge again."

"You didn't in Baker, John—oh yes, I've heard about it. It made the Kansas City papers. Just what are your plans? I understand you refused to be marshal of Broken Lance."

"I haven't any plans," Bonniwell replied. Suddenly he realized the emptiness of that statement. For days now he'd loafed about Broken Lance, the only man in the community who had no ambition, no desire to do anything or get anything.

He hadn't been contented during these weeks. He was an active man, normally. Idleness didn't make him happy. Someone on the street let out a wild whoop and fired his gun. Probably at the sky. It was a common occurrence. It made Bonniwell think of Jeff Barat.

He said: "I'll start in a half hour."

Twenty minutes later, Bonniwell led a sturdy Texas bronc to the hitchrail in front of Waggoner's office. A rifle butt stuck out of the scabbard; there was a blanket roll tied behind the saddle. Bonniwell looked through the window and saw Waggoner inside, shaking hands with a man.

Bonniwell waited until the man left. Then he went in and said: "I'm going away for a little while, Tom. Maybe two-three weeks."

Waggoner stared. "What?"

"Jim Westgard, the United States Marshal, has deputized me to get Doug Sutherland."

"Sutherland! Why, he was in Broken Lance the night before last. He and those cut-throats of his started a big fight, then lit out. I thought you were through with that sort of thing."

"That's what *I* thought. Got to do something, though."

"But why didn't you take the job of marshal of Broken Lance?"

"To be a walking target for every drunk in town?"

"Lee Thompson——"

"Won't be an old man. He's overdue already. In your place, Tom, I'd take a trip for a week or two myself."

"Can't, John. Too many things in the fire. There's a big herd on the way up from Texas, and I hear there's a flock of buyers and commission men coming to town in a day or two. But—you're coming back, aren't you?"

"Of course. And Tom, tell Lou I didn't have time to say good-by."

"It'd only take you a minute!"

"I'd rather not."

Bonniwell rode four blocks to the end of Main Street, crossed a little wooden bridge that had been hurriedly constructed over Indian Creek. Then he was among the Longhorns. As far as he could see, they covered the plains. Thousands upon thousands of them. Here and there a mounted cowboy, trying to keep his owner's animals from mingling with neighboring herds.

The Longhorns liked the short buffalo grass. Bonniwell thought the beeves, despite the nine hundred mile trip from Texas, in amazingly good flesh. This was good cattle country. In a few years the railroads would be going down into Texas. The herds would no longer come up here. A man could start a ranch of his own here then, be a thousand miles closer to the markets and get premium prices. Bonniwell played with the thought.

A man couldn't keep from thinking. You couldn't live on a ranch by yourself. Hired men were all right, but a ranch wasn't home without a woman around. You had to have an incentive to do things. By yourself, you could always get by. You could hunt buffalo, do a little trapping in the winter. But when you've had five bullets in you at one time and you've been in a hospital for seven or eight months, the zest for those things is gone. You think about settling down.

This was a good country. The Indians were pretty quiet. Soon, when the buffalo was gone, they'd stay on their reservations. The country would become civilized. When the railroad went farther south, the boom towns here would become quiet country villages. It would be much like Illinois around here.

Six miles south of Broken Lance, Bonniwell came upon a man doing a strange thing. He was plowing down the buffalo grass. Bonniwell stopped his horse and passed the time of day. Then he asked: "What you figure on raising here?"

"Wheat," the farmer replied. "This ground'll raise thirty-five, forty bushels of winter wheat to the acre."

"The first year, maybe," Bonniwell conceded, "but what if you get a good wind? It'll blow this top soil down to The Nations. You need that buffalo grass to hold it down."

"The buffalo grass don't bring any more," replied the farmer. "If the wind blows the farm away, all right. Plenty more land—it's free."

Bonniwell rode on. Two miles farther he met two Indians mounted on scrawny ponies. One of the Indians was naked save for a loin cloth, the other wore a loin cloth and above that a dirty pink shirt without a collar, but a flaming red necktie almost choking him. On his head was a battered Stetson.

Bonniwell kept his hands on the pommel of the saddle and stopped a dozen feet from the Indians. They regarded him sullenly in silence for a moment, then the man in the "white man's clothes" grunted, "Got tobac'?"

Bonniwell had a half dozen cigars in his shirt pocket. He took out two, tossed them to the Indians.

"More!" said the Indian with just the loin cloth.

"More, hell," Bonniwell replied.

The Indian with the Stetson had a rusty Sharp's rifle across his horse. He lifted it with his right hand in an angry gesture. Bonniwell knew that he had obtained that rifle from a buffalo hunter and that the hunter had not given it away willingly.

He smiled at the Indians and dropped his hands to his

sides. With the speed of light they came up, each holding a Frontier Model Colt. The righthand gun thundered and the Stetson leaped into the air. The Indians' ponies moved without urging. They departed.

Bonniwell rode on. Twelve miles from Broken Lance he came to a stage station, a sod house with a corral behind it. A whiskered Irishman was in charge. He was overjoyed when Bonniwell got down from his horse.

"B'gorra and I hope you stay the night with me. 'Tis lonesome here."

"Sorry, but I can't stay. Tell me, did four men ride past here yesterday?"

"Did they?" snapped the Irishman. "Come back to my corral and look at the crowbaits they left me, after taking four of my fine horses. You're the sheriff, maybe?"

"United States Deputy Marshal. That was Doug Sutherland and his gang. It's well you didn't try to fight them."

" 'Tis ashamed I am that I didn't! But domned if they didn't get the drop on me whilst I was lookin' away fer the minute."

"What time was it when they left here?"

"Just about this time. A mite later. The way they went they'll kill those horses."

Bonniwell frowned. For fifty miles or more the stagecoach trail went the way the outlaws were heading. Sutherland, if he wanted, could get fresh horses at every stage station. He could increase his twenty-four hour lead before leaving the trail to cut south into The Nations.

Bonniwell climbed back on his horse.

"Sure, an' you'll not be tryin' to capture them four by yourself?" cried the station man.

Bonniwell shrugged. "There'll be a break sooner or later. I'll be ready for it."

He camped beside a little stream that night. But he slept well away from it. He was up with the cold, dewy dawn. Before nightfall he left the stage route and headed straight south into the wild Indian country. He had a cold supper in the saddle and rode until long after dark. He slept only five hours and was in the saddle an hour before the sun came up.

He lost a little time cutting the trail, but when he found it, he grunted with satisfaction. He was less than twelve hours behind. He didn't lose any during the day.

It started to rain that night and before morning the rain turned to sleet. Bonniwell got under the shelter of an overhanging back and remained there all day, drenched to the skin. An ache developed in his left hip, where one of Sammy Taylor's bullets had once been embedded. He wrapped himself in a soggy blanket and shivered and dozed all night. The rain and sleet stopped before morning, but the sky was overcast and a raw, piercing wind came up.

The faint trail the outlaws had left was washed out. Bonniwell rode a zigzag course all day, but could not pick it up again. In the evening he made a fire, cooked bacon and coffee. He dried his damp blanket and clothes and slept soundly.

The sun awakened him.

He rode south until the sun was midway, then quit. Sutherland had changed direction during the rain. He might even have doubled back on his trail.

Bonniwell turned west. An hour later he had to take to cover in a small copse while a party of thirty Indians went by. They were Comanches, and Bonniwell did not like the way they traveled. They rode too stealthily.

He turned north for a few miles, then cut west again. In the afternoon of the third day following the rain and sleet he rode into the little town of Las Animas, Colorado. And there the hunch that had been riding with him became actuality.

He went into the Cattleman's Rest and found Leo Darby dealing faro to a lone player. When Bonniwell moved over to the table, Darby saw him and his eyes popped open.

"John Bonniwell!" He pushed back his chair and stuck out his hand. Bonniwell took it and the faro dealer pumped it vigorously.

"Hello, Leo," Bonniwell said. "How's things?"

"Rotten," exclaimed Darby. "Hell, there was a rumor that you were back, but I didn't believe it. I thought for sure you'd checked out at Haleyville."

Bonniwell smiled thinly. "It wasn't my time."

"I'm sure glad it wasn't. What are you doing here in Las Animas?"

Bonniwell shrugged. "Nothing particular. Like to have a drink with you when you get time."

"I was quittin' anyhow," said the faro player. He scooped

up his money and went to the door of the saloon. There he stopped, shrugged and turned back to the bar.

Bonniwell sat down at the table opposite Leo Darby.

"Seen Doug Sutherland in the last few weeks, Leo?" he asked.

Darby was one of the best gamblers in the Southwest. But the mere fact that he controlled his face so well told Bonniwell the answer.

"He's here," he said softly.

The faro player who had stepped to the bar, started for the swinging doors again. He walked sidewards, almost on his toes. Bonniwell shoved his chair to one side, said in a sharp voice, "Wait a minute!"

The man's face broke into a snarl and his hands, already hovering over his guns, went down. Bonniwell drew from a crouching position, an awkward one. The bullet from his gun hit the drawing man in the left shoulder and spun him completely around. One of his guns, already drawn, flew out of his hand, ricocheted from the roughhewn bar, and clanged against the sheet iron stove a dozen feet away.

The man fell against a chair, crashed it to the floor and slowly lay down himself. He did not move.

Bonniwell walked over to him and looked down. Then he turned to Leo Darby, still sitting at the table. "Who is he?"

"Jack Schiffkarten," said Darby.

The bartender's eyes were on Bonniwell, but he polished a glass. There were two patrons at the far end of the bar. They were very much absorbed in their drinks.

Bonniwell slipped his guns into their holsters, nodded and went out of the saloon. He stood on the wooden sidewalk in front of it, looked up and down the street. There were a dozen or so horses tied at the hitchrails. Across the street, diagonally, was a clump of four horses.

A couple of men came out of the general store near the horses, looked toward the Cattleman's Rest and talked together for a moment or two. Then one of them began rolling a cigarette and the other walked back into the store.

Bonniwell rested his shoulder lightly against a post of the wooden awning over the sidewalk in front of the Cattleman's Rest. He stuck a cigar in his mouth, but did not light it.

After awhile he realized that he was angry with himself.

He thought a moment about that anger and concluded that it was because of a familiar feeling. It always possessed him when there was impending action.

It wasn't a normal feeling. When a man knows he's about to be shot at, he ought to feel nervous, uneasy at least. He shouldn't feel ice in his veins. Because, hours later, there was reaction and it was not good.

But he knew, too, that no power on earth could make him leave his present post. No word of man, or deed, could force him to climb up on his mount and ride out of town. Not before the game was played out.

It was a long time coming. So long that Bonniwell could figure it all out. They'd heard the shot across the street, knew that Schiffkarten had been in the Cattleman's Rest. So they had come out and seen only one man leaning casually against a post in front of the saloon.

The man rolling the cigarette was holding Bonniwell's attention. The man who had gone back into the general store was going out through the rear. He would circle around, cross the street far above and hurry into the Cattleman's Rest through the rear. If the receiver of the fired bullet was really Jack Schiffkarten, well, they would have the man in front between them.

Bonniwell's ears were always supersensitive at these times. He heard boots clumping inside the Cattleman's Rest, but only a whisper of voices. He leaned against the post, but his shoulder scarcely touched it. Yet he was relaxed.

The man who had gone back into the general store came out again and started talking to his friend, who had finished rolling his cigarette and was lighting it. They walked to the group of horses.

A man who wears heavy boots and has lived all his life in the saddle cannot walk too lightly on tiptoe. The outlaw in the saloon made only a tiny, scraping noise, but Bonniwell heard it. He heard the man approach the batwing doors.

He did not hear the click of the hammer being cocked. The man had cocked it before entering the saloon in the rear. But he sensed the exact second when the outlaw was stretching himself to peer over the top of the batwing doors.

Then Bonniwell took one step to the right. His hands darted for his guns; he half turned and his right-hand gun roared death across his own stomach. He didn't even seem to turn back to the street, but his gun continued to thunder.

A horse screamed and plunged. A man was down on his knees, firing at Bonniwell. Bonniwell's right gun was empty and he made a shift with his left that did not even interrupt the thunder.

And then he stopped firing. The horse across the street broke away from the hitchrail, plunged wildly out to the street.

"Bonniwell?" called a voice inside the saloon.

Bonniwell did not turn. "Yes," he said.

Leo Darby came out and stood behind Bonniwell. He was breathing hoarsely, while he sized up the situation. Then he said, in a tone of awe, "You got them all."

Bonniwell was silent for a moment, then he dropped one Colt into its holster and began reloading the other. "It's surer than the United States Court," he said bitterly, "—and cheaper."

Chapter Nine

SIX-GUN LAW

MARK STONER SAID "Morning, Tom," to Waggoner and continued walking. Waggoner reached out and caught his arm. "Wait a minute, Mark."

Stoner grinned, but his forehead was creased. "Sure, Tom."

"What's this I hear about you selling your store, Mark?"

The creases on Stoner's forehead became deeper. "Uh, this Kansas City fella, Burlingame, made me a good offer and —well, I just sold it."

"I merely leased you the store property, for two years," Waggoner said.

"All right, Tom," said Stoner. "I had a bad run the other night. Jeff Barat offered me two thousand for the lease."

"So you sold it and promptly lost the money back to Barat. And now he's crowded you out of the store."

Stoner sulked. "I know I was a fool, Tom."

"You were, to believe Barat's games are honest. Well, good luck, Mark."

Jeff Barat was leaning against the doorpost of the Broken Lance Saloon & Dance Hall. He was smoking a black cigar.

"Morning, Mr. Waggoner," he said.

"You really figure on owning all of Broken Lance, eh, Barat?" Waggoner said bluntly.

Barat grinned. "Come inside a minute, Mr. Waggoner. Like to talk to you."

Waggoner followed the gambler through the big saloon into an office at the rear. He noted as they went through that Len Kelso was playing solitaire at a table. Kelso had reappeared the day before and no one had said a word to him about the killing of the Texas man in front of Josh Hudkins' Store.

Barat sat down at a desk in his office and from a drawer brought out a tin box.

"Some of the boys didn't figure leases were worth money, Mr. Waggoner," he said. "I bought up eight-ten of them pretty cheap."

"You could have paid more for them," said Waggoner, "and still won the money back at your games."

"That's right, but a couple of them might have doublecrossed me and taken the money to someone else's games." Barat rolled the cigar from the left side of his mouth to the right. "Mr. Waggoner, you can't fight our kind of money. In the long run my brother and I'll get you. But we like to do things quick. We'll pay you a hundred thousand dollars for all your holdings. A nice, clean sale."

"No," said Tom Waggoner.

"You didn't begin with more'n four-five thousand," said Jeff Barat. "That's a damn good profit. You've reached the top. In two months the cattle season'll be over and it'll be a long winter."

"Neither you nor your brother have enough money to buy me out," Tom Waggoner declared steadily. "Anyway, why should you waste a hundred thousand dollars? You could kill me much cheaper."

Jeff Barat's eyes glinted. "I don't like that kind of talk."

"Then don't insult me!" Waggoner clumped to the door of Barat's office. He opened it and said, "In the end Broken Lance will lick you, Barat."

Waggoner canvassed his leaseholders and learned the worst. Barat had worked it insidiously. Some of the merchants weren't yet aware that they were in the clutches of the Barats. Yes, they'd sold their leases, but they were running their stores just as usual.

"And you wouldn't even tell me before you sold it," Waggoner said bitterly to Ole Swenson.

"But hal, Tom," retorted Swenson. "There be twenty spec'lators in Broken Lance. You spec'late real estate yourself. I make little profit, so what I do?"

"You'll have to figure that out when Jeff Barat throws you out of this place and puts in one of his own men."

"He can't do dat," cried Ole Swenson.

"No," retorted Waggoner sarcastically. "But he will."

There were no customers in Lou Sager's shop, so Waggoner went in.

"The Barats have won another round," he told Lou. "They've been buying up my leases. I own a lot of stores, but Barat will run them. For a year or two, anyway, and after that I can have them again."

"I meant to warn you about that today," exclaimed Lou. "Jeff Barat's been awfully friendly to me lately. I thought it was because of Eleanor Simmons, but last night he offered me three thousand dollars for my lease. I thought it was such an absurdly high figure that I questioned him about it. I—I let drop that I didn't even have a lease and he shut up like a clam, then."

"Perhaps I'd better give you a lease," said Waggoner grimly.

"Tom!"

"Sorry," he apologized. "Barat's got under my skin. So has Broken Lance. You know, Lou, if I'd known what I was creating when I laid out Broken Lance for the railroad, I think I'd have bought all the land for twenty miles around the right of way and thrown the deed into the river."

"But the railroad's coming next week, and then they'll start shipping the cattle. Many of the Texas men will return home."

"Others'll take their place. There are now seventy-five thousand head of cattle on the plains around here. The drovers tell me at least that many more are headed here. And Broken Lance's reputation will get to them before they come near. The new lot of cowboys will be ready to pit themselves against Broken Lance. What we've seen the past week will be tame compared to what Broken Lance is going to see during the next two months. And tomorrow another issue of *The Point* comes out."

The Point came out the next day. On the first page was a scathing denunciation of the men of Broken Lance who were unfriendly to the "best interests of Broken Lance." At the end of the article was a list of names, with a subhead over it. *"The Enemies of Broken Lance."* There were eighteen names in the list. Tom Waggoner's name was first. He checked the list and discovered that the seventeen other names were of men who were lessees of his. None were men who had sold their leases to Jeff Barat. And Barat's name, of course, was conspicuous by its absence.

Waggoner got his guns, strapped them about his waist and went out to call on Mr. Monroe, the editor and publisher of *The Point*. He was still across the street, when he saw the little group converging upon the office of *The Point*. The group consisted of Lee Thompson, the marshal, his three deputies and Mayor Hudkins. Waggoner ran across the street and caught up with the tail end. Schumann, the chief deputy, saw him and turned.

He shook his head. "Better keep clear!"

Waggoner refused to heed him. He pushed past, into the office. Monroe was behind his desk and his two gunmen were just inside the door. But Lee Thompson quickly stepped in front of the gunmen.

"Just keep your hands still!" he ordered.

Hudkins stormed up to the editor.

"I'm closin' up your shop, Monroe!" he said.

"You try it——" blustered Monroe.

"I have. I got an injunction. Judge Stone. It's all legal. You don't get out another issue of this paper until it's settled in court. I'm suin' you personally for a hundred thousand dollars for slander——"

"Cut it!" snarled Lee Thompson.

One of the gunmen relaxed. Thompson's hands were on the butts of his .44's. He signaled to Schumann and the latter stepped around and flicked the guns out of the holsters of the guardians of *The Point*.

"I'm givin' you ten minutes to get out of town," Lee Thompson told the disarmed men.

"You'll save yourself a lot of trouble, Monroe," Hudkins said ominously, "if you'll take the same order."

"We'll see about that!" said Monroe, whitefaced. He got up, pushed through the little crowd and went out to the street.

Thompson reached down and yanked one of the gunfighters to his feet. He slammed him through the door. Schumann propelled the other man outside, although with a little more gentleness.

"That's that," said Mayor Hudkins grimly. "Either we have law and order in Broken Lance, or——"

The big window pane exploded into a million fragments. Thunder rolled into the newspaper shop and buckshot spattered over furniture and the men inside.

"Duck!" yelled Schumann, the deputy.

His command was unnecessary. Everyone in the room was already down. Lee Thompson, too. But he had not fallen of his own volition. His head was a mass of shredded bone and bloody flesh. He had taken the full blast of the shotgun.

A rifle roared and a slug crashed somewhere in the newspaper shop. A brace of pistols began stuttering. Schumann began crawling to the rear.

"The back way," he said.

"The hell with that!" cried Tom Waggoner. He started to get to his feet and a bullet tore at his coat sleeve. He promptly dropped back to the floor.

They retreated to the rear then, the three deputies, the mayor of Broken Lance and Tom Waggoner. In the alley they dispersed, Schumann and the deputies going one way and Hudkins and Waggoner another.

Main Street was strangely deserted when they reached it by a roundabout circuit of the block.

A jail had recently been built of solid logs. It consisted of one cell room on the first floor and a combination courtroom and marshal's office on the second.

Judge Stone was in the courtroom. He was the first lawyer to come to Broken Lance and had, by a vote of the city council, been elected judge. He was a somewhat seedy looking man of 35 or so, who enjoyed a poker game and liquor more than he did his judicial duties. At the same time, he was a sardonic, independent man with very strong convictions.

He fined cowboys a hundred dollars for disorderly conduct and at his first session fined the livery stable owner five hundred dollars for a similar offense. His contention was that a man should be fined according to his ability to pay.

"Lee Thompson's been killed," Hudkins told Judge Stone the minute he and Waggoner entered the courtroom. "I want a warrant for Jeff Barat's arrest."

"Barat kill Thompson?" asked the judge.

"Of course not. But you know he was behind it."

"No, I don't know it," said Judge Stone. "And unless you've got a strong case against him, I don't think I can issue a warrant for Barat."

Hudkins blew up. "Have you sold out to Barat? Who the hell do you think hired you?"

"The city council," said Judge Stone. "I guess they can fire me again if they want."

"You're damn right we can! And if you don't give me that warrant in a hurry, that's just what's going to happen."

"Easy, Josh," cautioned Waggoner. "You know that Judge Stone hasn't sold out to Barat. He gave you the injunction against *The Point*, didn't he?"

Hudkins glowered. "Yeah. Well, maybe you're right, Judge. But if we get somethin' on Barat——"

"I'll be only too glad to issue a warrant," snapped the judge. "You know, Hudkins, I don't give a damn for Barat. But what the hell could I do, even if you did bring him to this court? Could I sentence him to the penitentiary? You call me a judge, but I'm merely a local magistrate, without much legal authority. I can fine someone if your law officers can collect it, but that's about all. I can't send a man to the penitentiary. Only the higher court at Baker can do that."

"He's right, Josh," said Waggoner. "Anyway, who could serve a warrant now? Schumann——"

At that moment Schumann came in. He looked around the group. "Stimson and Paige have quit."

Hudkins gnashed his teeth. "Schumann, from now on you're marshal of Broken Lance. Hire yourself some deputies. As many as you think necessary."

"No," said Schumann. "I won't be marshal. I'll be a deputy, but I don't figure on being the main target for the guns around here."

Mayor Hudkins glared at Schumann. "Lose your nerve?"

Schumann looked down at his hands. "I've been scared stiff ever since I've been in Broken Lance. Haven't you?"

Before Hudkins could reply, Waggoner laughed. "I have."

Schumann nodded. "You need a marshal like Hickok or that young fellow Wyatt Earp who made Ben Thompson crawl into his hole in Ellsworth. Or John Bonniwell."

"Bonniwell's down in The Indian Nations," said Waggoner. "Anyway, he wouldn't take the job. It was offered to him."

"I think I'll take a vacation for a couple of weeks," said Schumann.

The boom of a shotgun rolled in through the window of the courtroom. Waggoner strode to the window, looked out upon Main Street. "Kelso's got a few of his friends together."

There were more than twenty. They had mounted horses and were riding up Main Street in the direction of the courthouse. Kelso was waving a double-barreled shotgun. Even as Waggoner looked he let go another blast at the sky. He followed it with a wild yell.

For two hours Kelso and his followers ruled Main Street. They rode from one end to the other, shot at the sky a few hundred times, sent a few bullets through store windows and yelled defiance to all of Broken Lance.

Jack McSorley still rode behind the buckboard when Eleanor Simmons went to Broken Lance. Arriving in Broken Lance, Eleanor gave Mose fifty cents and told him to be back at the buckboard in an hour. She shopped in a few of the stores, then went to Lou Sager's millinery shop to visit awhile.

Lou wasn't her usual cheerful self today.

"This town's gone crazy," she said. "It's as much as your life is worth to go out on the street."

"There's a bullet hole in your window, Lou," said Eleanor.

Lou shuddered. "Some of the cowboys think it's sport to break windows. I had three new panes put in during the past week."

Eleanor looked wide-eyed at Lou. "Did—did they shoot through the windows while you were in the store?"

"Of course. The mere fact that they might shoot a woman doesn't bother them any more. If things don't get better around here I'm going to sell—what are they up to now?"

The usual noise of mid-afternoon Broken Lance had risen to a tremendous crescendo. Lou walked nervously to the window and peered out.

"They're playing their new game," she said. "Some smart cut-throat invented it yesterday. They arm two Negroes with a bull whip apiece and let them whip each other. The one who quits first is the loser. The winner gets a huge prize—something like fifty cents."

Eleanor gasped. "But they might cut each other to ribbons with those awful whips."

"What of it? It doesn't hurt the men who put them up to it." She winced. "There they go!"

They could not hear the cracking of the whips inside the store, because the cowboys yelled too loudly. Eleanor covered her ears. But suddenly she heard Lou exclaim.

"Why, one of them is your man Mose!"

"Mose!" cried Eleanor.

"Yes, and he's getting the worst of it. It's—horrible!"

Before she realized what she was doing Eleanor was rushing from the store. Out in the middle of the street was a yelling, roaring, laughing crowd of three or four hundred men. In the center was a twenty-foot ring and in this stood the two Negroes, whaling away at each other with bull whips.

"Mose!" cried Eleanor. "Stop that."

Her voice was drowned by the roar of the crowd.

Eleanor clenched her fists and pounded the broad back of a cowboy.

"Let me through," she cried. "Let me through."

The cowboy turned and grinned at her. "Now, lady, this ain't the kinda thing you'd want to see."

"Of course it isn't, you fool!" screamed Eleanor. "One of them is my driver. I—want to make him quit."

"Why, sure, go right ahead." The cowboy, smiling broadly, stepped aside. But the men were pressed together twenty deep. It would have taken Eleanor ten minutes to force her way through. Meanwhile the cracking of the whips penetrated even the uproar of the wild audience.

Eleanor reeled back, dismayed.

And then a cool voice behind her said, "Go to Lou's store. I'll stop them."

She whirled and stared at John Bonniwell. He smiled crookedly and drew his long-barreled guns. Eleanor reached out to stop him. "No. Don't——!"

"It's all right," he assured her. He stepped around her, raised the muzzles of both guns to the sky and fired four quick shots.

The crowd promptly stampeded. Bonniwell, his guns thrust straight ahead of him, marched forward. Men fell aside, clearing a path for him to the Negroes, who stood now bleeding and scared, their whips trailing in the dust of Kansas Street.

"Beat it, you two," Bonniwell ordered. "And if I catch either of you doing this again I'll give you a beating you won't forget."

The Negroes dropped their whips and plunged into the milling crowd.

But now the half-drunken cowboys were beginning to understand that one mere man was robbing them of their sport.

"What the hell's the idea buttin' in?" one man yelled. He began tugging at his gun.

Bonniwell smiled icily at the man, took a step forward and smashed him along the temple with the long barrel of his gun. The man went down like a poled steer.

Bonniwell turned easily, swiveling his guns around with him.

"Anybody else want to make any objections?" he asked the crowd at large.

They didn't. They recognized him now. He was probably the only man in Broken Lance who could have got away with it.

"Bonniwell's back!" someone yelled. Men began to fall away. In a few minutes they were going to the saloons.

No one went near the unconscious man on the street. Bonniwell holstered his guns and stepped back.

"Where's the marshal?" he asked a man backing away from him.

The cowboy looked sullenly at him. "Ain't none."

So his prediction about the longevity of Lee Thompson's life had been accurate.

He was gone. He hadn't been told that Thompson was dead, but he knew it. Thompson had had more nerve than sense. And not quite enough stuff to back up his nerve.

He turned away to look for Eleanor. She had disappeared, gone back to Lou Sager's store, no doubt. But Tom Waggoner was running toward him now, coming from the direction of the courthouse.

"John!" Waggoner yelled.

John Bonniwell smiled his relief. These past few days he'd been thinking about Waggoner, a little afraid that he should not have left his friend in Broken Lance without his support.

They shook hands.

"I never was so glad to see you in my life!" declared Waggoner.

"Things been happening here, I gather," said Bonniwell.

"They have," said Waggoner vehemently. "For a week now Broken Lance has been hell. But come to my office. I've so many things to tell you."

They went to Waggoner's office. Bonniwell noted as they went in that the windows in front were broken.

"No use putting new ones in," said Waggoner. "They'd be broke again in a half hour."

Inside, Waggoner told Bonniwell of the things that had happened in Broken Lance during the past two weeks. *"The Point,* despite the injunction, came out with its third issue yesterday. It had a line across the top of the first page, "Order Prevails in Broken Lance." And right underneath, the editor printed a detailed list of the shootings and killings of the week.

"So Jeff Barat's taken over Broken Lance," said Bonniwell, thoughtfully.

"With a vengeance. He's calling a meeting of the town council for tomorrow morning, for the purpose of appointing Kelso as the new town marshal."

"What's he want to call the council together for?" asked Bonniwell. "He and his brother make only two of seven votes."

"No," said Waggoner. "The setup in Broken Lance has changed. The Barats have bought Beak Nelson. And Doug Fletcher was killed day before yesterday in a fight over a card game. You were away, which left only five men on the council. They would have outvoted Hudkins and myself."

"Now it's three and three. That makes a tie. Hm." Bonniwell was thoughtful for a moment. "You say they own Beak Nelson?"

"Jeff Barat bought his lease. If Nelson doesn't vote as Barat tells him, he'll be thrown out of his store."

"I see. Well, I guess we'll have to attend that council meeting."

Waggoner sighed in relief. "I feel better already. But tell me, John, how'd you make out on your trip? You got Sutherland?"

Bonniwell nodded. "In Las Animas."

"You didn't bring him back, though?"

Bonniwell's forehead creased slightly. "They didn't surrender."

Tom Waggoner whistled softly. After a moment he looked at his watch. "It's after five. I'm taking Lou to supper. Want to come along, John?"

Bonniwell shook his head, then suddenly changed his mind. "Yes, or rather, I'll meet you in the restaurant."

He left Waggoner at the door of the restaurant and went

inside. He passed up his usual place at a table against the wall and sat down near the window.

A couple of minutes later Waggoner appeared. With him were Lou Sager and Eleanor Simmons.

"John!" cried Lou Sager. "It's good to see you back in Broken Lance."

"I was glad to get back," he replied. His eyes were on Eleanor Simmons as he spoke.

"Mose is at the doctor's, so Lou insisted——" Eleanor tried to explain her presence.

"Kansas is agreeing with you," he said.

She flashed him a smile. "I didn't get to thank you for what you did outside a little while ago."

Lou Sager laughed. "What's on the menu? Beef steak or roast beef?"

Tom Waggoner chuckled. "Saw a man bring a bear in this afternoon. Ever try bear steak, Lou?"

She shuddered. "Goodness, no!"

Chapter Ten

"GIVE ME YOUR GUNS!"

BEFORE THE MEETING of the city council Ferdinand Barat gave earnest advice to his younger brother.

"We can show all our cards and wind up in a scrap. That's not the way to do it. We'll surrender to them, in the important things. Then they'll let us win a small victory. Our job'll be to build the little victory into a big one. You follow my lead, Jeff, and you'll see what'll come of it."

"All right," agreed Jeff Barat, "but I'm frank in saying I'm worried about John Bonniwell's return. The story's that he killed Doug Sutherland and his three men in a single-handed fight. The town's buzzing with the talk and I don't like it. Makes him too much of a hero to suit me."

"That's fine, Jeff, that's fine," said Ferd Barat, grinning craftily.

The council meeting this time was in the courthouse, which Judge Stone vacated.

The lineup of the factions was obvious in the seating arrangement, three on each side of the table that served as the judge's bench.

Mayor Hudkins opened the meeting. "Jeff Barat called this meeting. I figure he should do the talking."

"Before he does," said Ferd Barat, "I'd like to say a few words. It's obvious to all of us that Broken Lance has gotten out of control. Lawlessness and rowdiness are the order of the day. It is my idea that we need a law enforcement body headed by a man known for his courage. I want to propose that this council urge Mr. John Bonniwell to accept the post of marshal of Broken Lance!"

Tom Waggoner whistled in astonishment. Bonniwell, looking at Josh Hudkins at the moment, saw the merchant's eyes pop.

Bonniwell grinned crookedly. He said: "If the majority want me, I'll take the job."

The Barats and Doug Fletcher were as much surprised this time as were the others. The Barats had counted on John Bonniwell being adamant in his refusal and perhaps surrendering only after a long and serious appeal.

Tom Waggoner got over his astonishment quickly. Elated, he exclaimed: "I move that we vote on that."

It was a unanimous vote, of course.

"And now," Ferdinand Barat resumed, "I think the council should consider the matter of proper elections, both for the town of Broken Lance and the county. All of us hold offices by a flimsy private election, the legality of which is open to question. Broken Lance has become the most important town in the county. Unquestionably it will become the county seat. It is important therefore that we hold lawful elections as soon as possible."

Josh Hudkins looked about the group at the table. "What you say's true, Mr. Barat. For my own part I'm not stuck on the job of mayor. I'd rather someone who was regularly elected should have the job. It's a cinch his authority would be unquestioned then."

"Quite so, Mr. Hudkins," said Jeff Barat. "For my own part, I want to propose your name as a candidate for the office. I intend also to support you for the office."

Tom Waggoner nudged John Bonniwell. The latter knew that Waggoner was trying to guess what was behind Ferd Barat's apparent change of front.

Plans for the election were discussed. The Barats were

tractable to every suggestion that was made by the others. On one or two little matters they disagreed, but on slight argument conceded the point. The result of the meeting was that the Hudkins-Waggoner-Bonniwell faction won on all counts. Anyone in Broken Lance had the privilege of being a candidate for an office, provided a petition containing five percent of the estimated voting strength of Broken Lance was secured.

Two months ago John Bonniwell had told himself that he would never again use a gun against a fellow being, not for pay. Living in the West, he had to carry a gun. His life might depend on having one. But he would draw it only in self defense.

He hadn't wanted to be sucked into the maelstrom of frontier life. Yet he had been unable to avoid it. In Baker, on the first day of his return, had arisen an occasion when not his life alone, but the lives of others were at stake. He had used a gun to cow the drunken Texas men. While he hadn't fired it, he had nevertheless put himself in the position where he might have been compelled to use it.

The reaction had left him a little sick. But he thought it had merely strengthened his determination not to become again a professional gun wielder. Then his closest friend had asked him to ride shotgun on the stage that was carrying other friends. He had used a gun, effectively, even though it had been at long range.

And then Broken Lance. He had taken a passive interest in it, had remained merely because Tom Waggoner was in Broken Lance, because he thought Tom needed his moral backing. It wasn't because of Eleanor Simmons, he told himself, that he stayed in Broken Lance. No, it was because of Tom Waggoner. Eleanor had told him very plainly, in Baker, what she thought of him. That part of him was finished.

Yet because of a trifling incident concerning Eleanor Simmons he had accepted the deputation from Jim Westgard, had gone on a chase that was fraught with the utmost danger. He had faced gunfire again and had been victorious, as he always had been.

He had time to think things over then. Had finally and definitely faced the logical conclusion. *He was absolute master of any man on the plains with a gun.* It wasn't conceit. It wasn't because of any acquired skill. If a man grew to be seven feet tall, that was no feat of his own. It was in him. Some men may practice singing for ten years and never develop a voice. Another might sing in opera, without any training at all.

Bonniwell had the gift of guns. In a land and time when men practiced "the draw" daily to acquire proficiency, Bonniwell never touched his guns except to loosen them in the holsters now and then. Yet he could outdraw and outshoot the best. He had proved it time and again. That his talent was linked with a fatalistic coolness under danger was not unnatural. Without that quality his speed would not have developed.

Bonniwell was finally and reluctantly convinced that he was the right man for a certain task. He had really known it for weeks, but had not wanted to admit it even to himself.

Broken Lance needed a marshal. Not just an ordinary marshal. It needed John Bonniwell. He was the right man for the right job.

Bonniwell cleaned his guns in the back of Tom Waggoner's land office, oiled them and made sure there was no impediment in his holsters. Then he buckled the guns about his hips and tied the ends of the holsters to his thighs with buckskin thongs.

Tom Waggoner watched the procedure. "Maybe you were right before in not wanting to tackle the job. It's not a question of nerve any more. It's just that Broken Lance is out of hand."

"Do the drunks and thieves and ruffians own Broken Lance, Tom?" Bonniwell asked quietly, "or does it belong to you and Hudkins and all the other decent citizens?"

"I'm not arguing with you on that score," Waggoner smiled wanly. "It's just—well, you're the best friend I've got. And I'm worried about you. I can't for the life of me conceive how any man, even one like yourself, could quell the horde of thugs that have taken over Broken Lance."

"Well, I admit Haleyville at its wildest was only an imitation of Broken Lance, but I think I can handle this job. The first thing I'm going to do is enforce the ordinance against carrying guns inside the town limits."

Waggoner gasped. "You can't do that! Why, the Texas men would as soon give you their horses and saddles as their guns."

"They don't have to give them to me. They can check them

at the stores. If I can't get the cowboys and the others to disarm, I can't control Broken Lance. A gun is too much of a temptation to use if it's on a man's leg."

"But there are fifteen hundred Texas men in and around Broken Lance!" exclaimed Waggoner. "You can't make that many men disarm. Not if they ride in groups, as they usually do."

"I've got to do it, Tom," Bonniwell said seriously. "If I don't I can't win. I've got to make the Texas men realize that there is a law in Broken Lance, that the town isn't theirs, to do with as they like."

"All right," said Tom Waggoner slowly. "We'll organize a committee to back you up in any emergency."

"No, a committee can't rule Broken Lance. It's got to be one man. All I want you to do, Tom, is see that printed copies of the gun-toting ordinance are put up in conspicuous places about town."

"They'll be up this evening. And, John——" Waggoner stopped. He nodded at his friend.

The news that John Bonniwell had been appointed marshal of Broken Lance was known before he took the street. He passed men and they stopped to look at his back. On the other side of the street, they congregated in small groups and stared at him as he passed along.

The saloons were the logical centers for the checking of the cowboys' guns. Bonniwell went into them and talked to the proprietors.

"The cowboys are going to start checking their guns in town," he told Humphrey Small, who owned the San Antone Bar, "it'd be a good idea if you'd rig up a bunch of nails on the wall behind the bar, to hang the guns."

"You're going to try to enforce a law like that?" Humphrey Small asked in astonishment.

"I'm *going* to enforce it," said Bonniwell. "They can come into town with their guns and they can ride out with them, but they can't carry them while they're in Broken Lance. Not after today."

"You're the marshal," said Small. "I'm just a saloon keeper. If any men want to check their guns with me, I'll do it. But I can't make them do it."

"You don't have to. They'll want to do it of their own accord."

Bonniwell talked to four other saloon proprietors. Their reaction was much like that of Humphrey Small. He avoided the saloons that were owned or controlled by Jeff Barat.

On his way back from his trip up the street, Bonniwell saw Tom Waggoner nailing a white notice on the outside of the office of *The Broken Lance Point*. Before Waggoner could walk away a dozen cowboys came from the Broken Lance Saloon & Dance Hall next door and surrounded Waggoner. Bonniwell could hear them jeering at his friend.

Well, it was as good a time as any to start. Probably better than later, when the cowboys had had too much time to talk things over and fortify themselves with liquid defiance.

He crossed the street diagonally. When he was halfway across the group about Waggoner spied him and spread out to face him. Bonniwell raised his eyes so they were focused on the awning over the newspaper office. He kept them there until he was on the wooden sidewalk directly in front of the Texas men.

Then he brought his eyes down and ran them slowly over the group. He stopped when his eyes came to a snarling face.

"You've read the sign, cowboy?" Bonniwell asked carelessly.

"Yeah, and I'd like to see *anyone* make me give up my guns!" exclaimed the Texas man.

Bonniwell's mouth twisted in a half smile. He held out his left hand.

"Give me your guns," he said.

It was the challenge. The Texas man had been singled out of the group for the test. He had made the boast and been challenged. It was up to him now to buckle down to Bonniwell, or do something about it.

For a second the Texas man was as still as death. Then he went for his guns.

No man there could have said that he saw John Bonniwell's right hand shoot for his gun. But all knew that suddenly the sun was flashing on metal and that Bonniwell was lunging forward.

He didn't shoot. If he had he wouldn't have lunged forward. But he laid the long barrel of his Frontier Model Colt along the left temple of the Texas man's head with a force that sent the man reeling back into the arms of his comrades.

The Texas man's gun didn't even clear leather. It was still

in his holster when he ricocheted from the surge of his friends and slithered to the wooden sidewalk in front of the newspaper office.

Then Bonniwell stepped back. His gun was in his hand, held carelessly with the muzzle drooping.

"Does anyone else want to *make* me take his guns?" he asked.

No one said a word. But every man there breathed heavily. Again Bonniwell picked out a leader. "You," he nodded to a whiskered giant. "Take off your guns and drop them to the sidewalk."

With his eyes fixed on Bonniwell's in a hypnotic stare, the big Texan unbuckled his gunbelts and let them fall about his feet.

"The rest of you," Bonniwell ordered.

Every man of them obeyed. Bonniwell swept the guns together with his foot and pushed the heap to one side toward Tom Waggoner.

"Take them to your office, Tom," he said. "The men can have them when they leave town."

"You mean that?" one of the Texans found voice to ask.

"Of course. They're your guns. The city ordinance merely forbids you to carry them while in town. Beginning tomorrow there'll be a dozen places where you can check your guns when you come in to Broken Lance."

Bonniwell slid his own gun back into his holster. Then he stooped and twisted his hand into the collar of the unconscious Texas man's coat. Turning his back upon the group, he began dragging the man down the street.

All of Broken Lance, it seemed, was lined along the sidewalks. So that all could see him clearly, Bonniwell took to the middle of the street.

He dragged the unconscious man carelessly, even swerving a little to pull him through a small mud puddle. He wanted the lawless element in the town to see what happened to a man who dared to defy the law of Broken Lance.

Before he got to the stout courthouse and jail Henry Schumann came out of a store and joined him.

"I just got back from a vacation, Mr. Bonniwell," he said. "Wonder if you're looking for a deputy?"

Bonniwell let go of the unconscious man.

"I am," he said, "and you're hired. Take this to jail and see that he stays there until tomorrow morning."

"Judge Stone's in court now."

"A night in jail will take the fight out of a man," said Bonniwell. "We'll take them to trial only once a day." Without waiting to see the disposition of the man who had defied him, Bonniwell returned down the street. He walked on the opposite side from the newspaper office this time. But he walked leisurely. He wanted to give everyone a chance to see him, to make any protest they felt entitled to make.

Josh Hudkins was standing in his doorway.

"Fine work, John!" he praised.

Bonniwell nodded. In the door of the bank stood Jeff Barat and his bodyguard. When they saw Bonniwell coming they turned and went inside.

In the window of her shop Lou Sager signaled to Bonniwell. But he shook his head slightly and continued to Tom Waggoner's office.

Inside, he found Waggoner slumped in his chair, perspiration standing out on his forehead.

"You got away with it!" he said.

"Once," replied Bonniwell. "And now the rest of the day they're going to talk it over. And some of them are going to dare each other to resist. There'll be a showdown either tonight or tomorrow."

Tom Waggoner groaned. "Oh, Lord! I thought you were a goner that time. Why didn't you shoot that cowboy? You had every occasion to do so. He was drawing——"

Bonniwell's eyes slitted thoughtfully. "A real bad man doesn't like to be buffaloed and dragged to the calaboose. He figures a thing ought to be settled with bullets. My idea is to humiliate the bad man. I think the lesson will take better."

"I don't want to see your next lesson," Waggoner shuddered. "I'm a nervous wreck now."

Bonniwell had an early supper at the Trail City Restaurant. He ate heartily and lit up a cigar afterwards. He strolled down the street puffing easily on the cigar. He had to pass Lou Sager's store, but avoided looking in. He did not want to talk to Lou—yet.

Tom Waggoner was gone from the office when Bonniwell returned. He found a copy of this week's *Point* and read it from first page to last. The reading consumed more than an hour. He looked at his watch then and found that it was six-thirty. Still too early. He went to his cot behind the partition and stretched out on it. He actually dozed.

When he awoke it was dark in the office. He did not strike a light. He tried his guns to see that they were not stuck in the holsters.

He went into the light-studded darkness of Kansas street. He knew that it was quite possible there was a man or two hiding in the gloom who might take a shot at him. He couldn't help that. He had to take the risk. He walked across the street to Jeff Barat's main saloon.

When he hit the sidewalk his ears told him that the revelry inside the big dance hall and saloon was somewhat modified tonight. He had expected it to be. He pushed open the batwing doors and in his first glance saw that the stage was set for him. The saloon and dance hall was crowded; the games were playing to capacity; but there was a rather wide aisle from the door to the seventy-five foot bar. And at the closest end of the bar stood Len Kelso, Slingerland, and Jeff Barat.

Jeff Barat wore his flowered waistcoat and the Prince Albert with the velvet collar. There was a long black cigar in his mouth. No guns showed on his hips.

But there were guns on the other two men.

Bonniwell was spotted instantly. No one said a word, but a hush ran through the saloon. Bonniwell walked steadily down the lane that had been left for him, until another step would have collided him with Jeff Barat. Then he stopped.

"You men read the city ordinance about carrying guns," he stated, rather than asked.

"We read it," said Kelso, shortly.

"We're packin' our guns," Slingerland added.

Bonniwell nodded. Out of the tail of his eye he saw the look-out at the faro table, slowly swing sidewards, so his left hand was concealed from Bonniwell. But Bonniwell knew what the hand held.

He smiled pleasantly and dropped his eyes to Len Kelso's midsection. Then with the smile still on his face he smashed a terrific blow at Jeff Barat. It caught the big gambler completely by surprise.

The blow hit Barat high on the left side of his face and knocked him sidewards into Kelso, throwing the latter off-balance, even as he was going for his gun.

Bonniwell followed through on the punch. He took two quick steps to the right and behind Barat. He drew his right gun as he moved and when he came behind Barat he slugged him over the head with the barrel of the gun. Barat sagged forward, but Bonniwell whipped his left hand about his waist and kept him from slumping to the floor.

The lookout's gun thundered and a bullet crashed into the back bar mirror. Bonniwell, his smile now twisted into a snarl, stabbed out with his gun, around Barat's body and jammed it into lean Slingerland's spine.

"Up with 'em!" he said savagely.

Slingerland yelped and arched away from the gun. Bonniwell rammed it again into his spine.

"You, Kelso!" he said. "Drop your gun or Slingerland and Barat both get it!"

Kelso's guns were clear of his holsters. He was turning to shoot Bonniwell. But when he saw the turn the situation had taken he stopped. His eyes blazed with hate and anger, but his mouth was open in surprise.

"Damn you!" he said thickly.

"Drop the guns," Bonniwell ordered. "And that goes for the lookout and anyone else around here who has ideas. Drop 'em quick!"

It was the only thing Kelso could do. Slingerland's life he might have risked, but not Jeff Barat's. Barat was his employer. Without him, Len Kelso would not even have been tolerated in Broken Lance.

When his guns clattered to the floor, John Bonniwell gave the unconscious body of Jeff Barat a violent shove that threw it against Len Kelso. Then he whipped out his other gun. And with two guns in his hands there wasn't a man in the saloon who would risk drawing.

"All right, you two," Bonniwell said to the disarmed gunfighters. "Pick up your boss and carry him to the calaboose." He could almost hear the gasp that went up in the saloon, but he did not turn his eyes away from the men before him.

Slingerland half turned around. His guns were in his holsters and there was a look of inquiry in his eyes. Bonniwell refused to heed it. He made a gesture at Jeff Barat.

They picked him up, then, Kelso the shoulders and Slingerland the ankles. And so they carried him out of the saloon, Bonniwell marching behind. No one followed. Not right away.

But when they were halfway down the street, Bonniwell heard men stamping around in the dark. They were yet twenty feet from the calaboose when the voice of Ferdinand Barat called out from behind.

"Mr. Bonniwell—wait!"

There was a light in Judge Stone's court. The door was thrown open and Henry Schumann came out on the little porch at the head of the stairs. He peered down into the darkness and whistled. Immediately behind him appeared Tom Waggoner.

He called out, "John?"

"Yes," replied Bonniwell. "Henry, come down and unlock the jail. I got a couple of customers for you."

Schumann took the stairs two at a time. Quickly he unlocked the padlock on the jail door and yellow light from inside flooded the group near the entrance.

"Slingerland's still got his guns," said Bonniwell. "Get them."

Ferdinand Barat pounded up from the rear.

"Mr. Bonniwell, what have you done to my brother?" he demanded.

Bonniwell half turned. He saw that the banker was unarmed and slipped his own guns into their holsters.

"I buffaloed him," he said, shortly.

"But what are you going to do now?" cried Ferd Barat. "You can't—throw him in jail!"

"Watch!" said Bonniwell. "All right, Schumann, in they go. All three of them!"

Schumann hustled the prisoners into the jail, to join the man Bonniwell had arrested in the afternoon. He pulled the door shut and took the padlock in his hand to snap it in the hasp.

Barat leaped around Bonniwell and rushed at the deputy. "You can't do that!"

Schumann rammed his elbow into the big banker's stomach.

"Don't monkey with the law!" he snapped.

Ferd Barat staggered back. Then he reached under his Prince Albert and brought out a .41 derringer.

"Give me that key!" he cried.

Bonniwell chopped down with his fist on the banker's forearm and the little gun flew out of his hand.

"Carrying guns, Mr. Barat?" he cried. He seized the corpulent banker by the scruff of his Prince Albert, kicked the jail door open with his foot and threw Ferd Barat bodily inside. Then he reached in and drew the door shut with a slam. He took the padlock from Henry Schumann's hand and snapped it shut himself.

"That's that," he said, grimly.

Tom Waggoner was behind Bonniwell by this time.

"Gawd!" he breathed.

The three of them climbed the stairs to Judge Stone's court. There were a couple of shotguns and a .50 caliber Sharp's rifle in a rack. Bonniwell examined the guns to see that they were loaded.

"I guess I'll stay up here tonight," he announced, "just in case any of the Barats' friends get a notion to break them out of jail."

Tom Waggoner was pacing the floor. "D'you think you did the right thing, arresting the Barats, John? After all, they are about the wealthiest men in town."

"All the more reason to arrest them. Jeff Barat put Slingerland and Kelso up to wearing their guns. He had a trap rigged up for me. It's only right that I arrested him. And his brother —well, he assaulted an officer of the law. I figure we got an easier chance to enforce the law in Broken Lance if we prove that it treats everyone equal, if he's a busted cowboy from Texas or the leading citizen of Broken Lance."

In that Bonniwell was right. The three of them, Schumann, Waggoner and Bonniwell remained in the courtroom all night. There was no disturbance outside. Broken Lance, it seemed, retired earlier than usual.

And the next day men began going about Broken Lance without their guns. Bonniwell had won a victory—a temporary one, at least.

At ten o'clock, when Judge Stone opened court, the room was crowded with spectators and there were a hundred men or more outside. Bonniwell stood at the top of the stairs just outside the courtroom, while Schumann went down and brought up the five prisoners.

Jeff Barat came up first. His face was bitter and his eyes ringed. He had not slept in the calaboose. His brother followed him, still corpulent and dignified, but in need of a shave. He walked haughtily past John Bonniwell.

"Court called to order," announced Judge Stone, banging on the table with a small hammer.

Schumann herded the prisoners so they were lined up before Judge Stone's table.

"What's the charges?" the judge asked.

"For these three," Bonniwell said, indicating Kelso, Slingerland and the Texas cowboy who had been buffaloed the afternoon before, "carrying firearms in violation of the city ordinances."

"Guilty or not guilty?" asked the judge.

"Guilty," said the Texas man. Kelso and Slingerland looked at one another, then Kelso said gruffly, "Not guilty."

"Guilty," said Judge Stone. "Twenty-five dollars or twenty-five days in jail. Next."

"Jeff Barat is charged with inciting to riot," Bonniwell charged. "His brother, Ferd—attacking an officer of the law."

"Guilty or not guilty?"

"I protest this high-handed . . ." began Ferd Barat, blusteringly.

Judge Stone pounded on his table with the hammer. "Guilty. One hundred dollars fine, each of you. Pay or go back to jail."

"The hell with you!" cried Jeff Barat.

"Fifty dollars more—contempt of court!" snapped the judge.

Ferd Barat caught his brother's arm.

"We'll pay the fine," he said. He pulled out a huge roll of greenbacks and paid their fines.

"Court adjourned," barked Judge Stone.

It was a big county, yet, save for the scattered settlers, there were only two centers of population—Baker, at the northern end of the county, and Broken Lance, almost a hundred miles southwest.

Baker had been the big town, but was now on the decline. Broken Lance was in the ascendancy. It should, if for no other reason than bulk of population, elect the county officials. The voters of Broken Lance were confident of that.

Yet when the necessary candidates' petitions were filed, Bonniwell discussed them with Tom Waggoner. "They've put Jim Malachy, of Baker, up for sheriff. How do they figure to elect him?"

"They don't, I guess," said Waggoner. "Any more than they can hope to put across Olcott for judge. I really think you should have run for sheriff, though. Schumann's a good man and well known, but you'd draw the Baker votes. They remember how you bluffed Malachy."

"Being marshal of Broken Lance is job enough for me," said Bonniwell. "And as far as Baker's concerned, watch it. Something about their setup smells."

His intuition was uncanny. The day before election, *The*

Broken Lance Point came out with a strong appeal for the Baker candidates for the county offices.

"We should have kept that injunction on *The Point*," complained Waggoner. "A big bundle of those papers went to Baker on the stage."

"I see the fine hand of Jeff Barat in this. And I think it would be a mighty good idea to send five or six good Broken Lance men to be at the Baker poll, right through the counting of the ballots."

"They'll start in ten minutes!" declared Waggoner.

There were two polling places in Broken Lance, one in the Barat Brothers Bank and the other in Josh Hudkins store. Three men besides the regular election officials were assigned to guard the ballot boxes. And John Bonniwell spent the day going from one polling place to another.

The voting was done with a surprising degree of quietness. It worried John Bonniwell. He was still not relieved in the evening when the ballots were counted and the results posted.

For Sheriff: Henry Schumann, 456;
   Jim Malachy, 98.
For Judge: William Stone, 540;
   George Olcott, 14.

The Broken Lance offices were practically unopposed and Josh Hudkins was re-elected mayor.

It looked like a victory for Broken Lance, but Bonniwell, retiring early, was up with the dawn. A half hour later, four of the six Broken Lance men who had gone to Baker to watch at the polls, returned. One of the four had a bandage about his shoulder.

He knew before Pete Jasper told him: "Every damn Texas man in Baker voted. Jim Malachy got 1800 votes. Olcott the same."

Bonniwell sighed. "You tried to keep the Texas cowboys from voting?"

"You'll notice Zwing and Hunter ain't with us," Pete Jasper retorted. "They're buryin' 'em today."

Bonniwell awakened Waggoner and told him the news. Waggoner was fighting mad. "We'll declare the Baker ballots illegal."

"How? Baker's proud. The citizens are mad because Broken Lance has passed them. They'd fight to the last man. You'd have a civil war if you went to Baker with an armed force. Besides, it isn't so bad. We still control Broken Lance."

"But neither Olcott and Malachy like you." Waggoner grunted. "Funny, that two men who were once such enemies should now be working together."

"Politics make strange bedfellows. Malachy can't go back to Texas because of the warrants that are out for him down there. Being sheriff up here is a good sport for him. An' being county judge is more profitable than being mayor of a dying trail town."

"Do you think they'll make their headquarters in Broken Lance?"

Bonniwell shrugged. "I don't know."

They found out before noon. Olcott, Malachy and a half dozen retainers rode into Broken Lance. They went to the Barat Brothers Bank and remained there for a half hour. Then word came out that Judge Olcott would make his headquarters in Broken Lance, but Jim Malachy would return to Baker. He would be represented in Broken Lance by a deputy sheriff, whom he was appointing.

The deputy sheriff was Len Kelso, Jeff Barat's chief lieutenant and executioner.

A little while later Kelso came into the Broken Lance courthouse. Bonniwell was sitting in a chair behind a desk. Kelso grinned wolfishly.

"This is county property."

"Broken Lance money built it," said Bonniwell.

"Yeah, but we made a dicker with the mayor. Broken Lance uses the jail for temporary prisoners. The county of Baker gets the court room and these nice upstairs offices."

Bonniwell got up and went out. He walked down the street to Josh Hudkins' store.

"The county officers have taken over the courthouse," he told the mayor.

Hudkins' forehead creased. "Couldn't help it. I was just talkin' to Tom. He thinks we ought to build an addition to the place. We still have Judge Stone as justice. He tries all small cases—civil cases, involving not more than one hundred dollars."

"I'll use Tom's office as my headquarters for a while," said Bonniwell. "That is if I'm still marshal."

"Of course, John!" cried Hudkins, quickly. "We'd be lost without you."

"I wonder," said Bonniwell and went out.

A Texas man was sheriff of Baker County and a notorious

gunfighter was deputy sheriff, with headquarters in Broken Lance. Kelso drew wages from the county of Baker, and regular pay from Jeff Barat, a saloon and bordello proprietor.

In Broken Lance John Bonniwell ruled, but a man could commit a murder in Broken Lance and, by making a dash outside the town limits, be safe from molestation, provided it suited the purposes of Jeff Barat to have him unmolested.

It didn't take the transient citizens of Broken Lance long to learn that. Two days after Kelso took over as deputy sheriff, a Texan under the influence made a test of the new setup.

He went into Josh Hudkins' store and asked for a left-handed monkey wrench. Hudkins wasn't in the mood for joking that morning and snapped sourly at the cowboy. Whereupon the cowboy reached into his shirt and brought out a short-barreled Colt. He took a shot at Mr. Hudkins' right ear and drew blood. Hudkins dropped down behind the counter and the cowboy, not wanting to exert himself, went outside. Men were coming out of the stores and saloons to see what the shooting was about. The cowboy looked up and down the street, let out a defiant whoop and sent a bullet or two crashing through the windows of the Golden Prairie Saloon across the street.

He timed things very nicely. A block away John Bonniwell dashed out of a store. The cowboy whooped and made a jump for his horse, which he had very conveniently tied to the hitchrail in front of the store. He got out of town before Bonniwell could commandeer a mount.

Bonniwell didn't think that it would do any good, but he looked up Deputy Sheriff Kelso.

"I want to swear out a warrant for a cowboy named Striker," he said.

"Yeah? What's the charge?"

"Disorderly conduct, carrying firearms in violation of city ordinance——"

"Striker's in Broken Lance now?"

"Of course not. You know damn well he rode out of town."

"In that case there's not a thing I can do about it. There's no county or state law forbidding a man to carry a gun."

"What about intent to kill?"

Kelso scratched his chin. "All right, I'll get out the warrant, but what good you figure it'll do? This is a big territory and I'm the only deputy sheriff around. I can't be expected to arrest every petty law violator. I've got a lot of things to take care of, and if it ain't a serious charge I might forget——"

"All right, forget all about it," said Bonniwell. "I just wanted to make sure."

Kelso grinned derisively. "And make sure too, Bonniwell, you don't try arresting anyone outside the city limits of Broken Lance. You're marshal of this town, but outside of it you ain't got any more to say than any cowboy from Texas."

Bonniwell walked out of the deputy's office. Thereafter he kept a horse saddled and tied to the hitchrail in the center of town. It didn't work, however. The cowboys spotted his horse and made sure to commit their depredations far enough away, so they could gain their horses and make a safe getaway. Two more shot up the town that afternoon and took to their horses.

Waggoner had a couple of real estate prospects and was out in the country with them. Around five o'clock John Bonniwell stopped in at Lou Sager's shop and asked her to have supper with him at the Trail Restaurant. She accepted readily.

Seated in the restaurant, Lou rested her elbows on the table and folded her hands together. Then she rested her chin lightly on her hands and looked at John Bonniwell across the table.

"Remember when we first met, John—on the train?"

He nodded. "I guess I was pretty surprised at the idea of a girl starting a millinery shop out in this country."

"You practically told me I was crazy." Lou smiled. "Well, I've made good. I've got enough money to bring my mother out here. She's coming in a couple of weeks."

"Say, that's fine!" he exclaimed. But he couldn't quite conceal the little crease on his forehead. Lou saw it and said quietly:

"You don't think I should bring her yet?"

He looked down at the table for a moment. Then he said: "No. Broken Lance is heading for a blow-off. I hope it'll be delayed until the cowboys leave next month. But I guess that's expecting too much. Wait until——"

"I'd like to see her. Broken Lance is a lonesome place, you know."

"I know. Not much fun for a girl like you. At that, it's better than being on a ranch with no other woman around at all."

"You mean I'm better off than Eleanor Simmons?"

He frowned. He hadn't meant to talk about Eleanor. He

shook his head quickly and tried to change the subject. He plunged into another delicate one. "Tom's out selling a farm. There's a man, Lou, whom it'll be worth watching. He's going to be one of the biggest men in this state one of these days."

"I know he is. I'm not worrying about Tom at all. But you—where'll you be in ten years, John?"

He shrugged. "I don't know. I never gave it much thought."

"But I have, John."

In panic, Bonniwell exclaimed, "Are you going to the dog races next Sunday?"

Lou Sager sighed. "I go to all the dog races, all the horse races and all the shooting matches. I think you're blind, John."

Chapter Eleven

FRAMED

"Jeff," said Ferdinand Barat, "we're licked."

Jeff was startled. "Licked? What do you mean?" He held up his hand, palm upwards, the fingers crooked like claws. "I've got Broken Lance like this. Anytime I want to I can close my hand on it."

"And what'll you get?" The older Barat pulled a slip of paper from his pocket. "I was doing some figuring today, Jeff. Let me read this to you. We got beat on the building lots in Broken Lance. What we own cost us in the neighborhood of $75,000. The two or three building lots we own outside cost us another $25,000."

"Sure," exclaimed Jeff. "But they're worth all that or more."

"Are they? You bought up a bunch of Waggoner's leases. I loaned money to folks we figure we can squeeze. All right—we're two hundred thousand dollars in the red. In the credit column we've got a lot of scattered holdings. We can push around a lot of people who don't amount to anything. We've practically ruined the cattle business for Broken Lance. *You* did that, Jeff. In a month, the cattlemen will stop coming here. Chances are they won't come next year. So we'll have a lot of property with no chance to make anything off of it."

Jeff Barat gnawed at his knuckles. "There are just three people who've spiked our plays right along. Waggoner, Bonniwell and Ollie Simmons."

"That's what I was getting to," said Ferd Barat. "We need Waggoner's holdings in town. But even more than that we need those five thousand acres of Simmons. Remember that business you told me about in New York—charging these cattle people for grazing permission? That never worked at all. And yet that's one of the things we counted on most."

Jeff Barat sulked. "You've made Simmons a dozen propositions and he's laughed at all of them."

Ferdinand Barat folded his hands and cracked his knuckles. "There's one way to get to him, Jeff. A bullet."

Jeff snapped, "How're you going to shoot a man who's always got fifty of the toughest men in the country around him? When he comes to Broken Lance there are never less than a dozen men with him."

"There is only one way to get to Ollie Simmons, and that's through that niece of his."

Jeff grinned wolfishly. "Do you think I've been asleep? Don't you think I've tried to make love to her?"

"Have you?" asked his brother. "I haven't heard the sound of wedding bells."

Jeff scowled, "Bonniwell again. She's crazy about him. She talks to me and all the while she's thinking of John Bonniwell. When she's walking down the street with me she's looking around to see him. Every time there's a shot goes off in Broken Lance she's afraid it's Bonniwell getting hurt."

Ferdinand Barat stabbed his forefinger at Jeff. "Ah, that's something. Work on it a minute."

Jeff worked on it, but he didn't like it.

"I'm not afraid of many things in this world," he said grimly. "But I don't mind telling you I'm not awfully happy at the thought of facing Bonniwell's guns."

Eleanor Simmons came into Broken Lance with her usual escort of Mose, the driver, and Jack McSorley. She would just as soon have done without McSorley. The foreman had been acting strange lately. He spent altogether too much time about the ranchhouse, and the moment Eleanor moved away from it more than fifty feet he somehow materialized and managed to get into her path.

As yet he had made only the barest advances, but Eleanor was a woman and understood McSorley by instinct.

He was a rather noisy man in the company of the cowboys. Eleanor knew from things her uncle had let drop that McSorley was a reckless sort of a man, quick to fight and a formidable man when roused.

Yet when he rode behind Eleanor's buckboard he was glum and silent. He was unusually morose today, not speaking a word during the entire eight-mile ride.

Eleanor left him at the buckboard and went into Hudkins' store to make some purchases. When she came out, McSorley was still at the buckboard.

"I won't be ready to go home for another hour, Jack," she told him. "Why don't you enjoy yourself in the meantime?"

"Nothin' much I enjoy doin' in Broken Lance," he replied.

"What?" she exclaimed laughingly. "Have you reformed?"

He grinned feebly, but was quickly sober again. "A man gets tired of drinkin' and gamblin' after a few years. Besides, I been doin' a lot of thinkin' lately."

She could see his face tighten suddenly and knew what he was leading up to. She backed away, hurriedly. "Don't—think too much, Jack!"

She turned and walked quickly to Lou Sager's millinery shop. At the door she looked back and caught his eye. He was still standing by the buckboard.

Lou Sager took her hands when she entered the store.

"I wish you could get to town oftener!" she exclaimed.

"So do I, Lou," Eleanor replied. "Uncle Ollie doesn't like me to come in too often. He worries, as it is."

"It's safe enough," sighed Lou. "Or it has been. That's one thing about those wild Texas men. They don't molest women, anyway."

"At that, I feel safer at the ranch," said Eleanor. "If it only weren't so lonely out there."

"It's just as lonely here. That's why I wish you lived in town. But next week we're going to have a real celebration. The Reverend Fellows—remember that minister who came to Broken Lance on the stage with us? Well, he's going to build a church."

"For who?" exclaimed Eleanor.

Lou laughed. "Strangely, there are a few people in this town who'd like a church. Anyway, the Reverend Fellows is

115

having a bazaar next week. A regular old-fashioned church bazaar. He hopes to raise enough money to build the church. Tom Waggoner has given him the land. You *must* come to the bazaar, Eleanor. All the elite of Broken Lance will be there."

"The elite?" asked Eleanor mockingly. "Mr. Buckshot Roberts, the Honorable Buffalo Tom, Squire Cherokee Bill——"

"And perhaps Snake Thompson and One-Shot Mulligan," Lou added. "But it will be fun. Our first real social event. It's Wednesday evening."

"I'll make Uncle Ollie bring me," said Eleanor. "Is Tom Waggoner going?"

Lou's eyes wrinkled a little. "He's asked me to go with him."

"That's fine." Eleanor smiled. "Uncle Ollie thinks a lot of Mr. Waggoner. Say's he's the sort of man this country needs."

"Yes," agreed Lou. "Tom's fine. He's manly, he's got initiative and he's handsome. His disposition is wonderful. He's everything a woman could want—I guess."

Eleanor inhaled softly. "Guess?"

"No, I don't guess," Lou said soberly. "I know he is. I'm proud of him. He's asked me to marry him."

"And you haven't accepted him?"

"I haven't accepted him. Ten times a day I call myself a fool. Three or four times a day I see him passing this store and every time my heart twists—and I can't say yes to him."

"Why not, Lou?" Eleanor could have bitten off her tongue for asking the question, yet no power on earth could have prevented her.

Lou Sager's eyes met Eleanor's steadily. "I can't marry Tom Waggoner, because I'm in love with John Bonniwell. I—I guess you knew that, Eleanor."

Eleanor's face was white and she scarcely breathed. "Yes—I knew."

"And John's in love with you."

Eleanor did not reply. She wished suddenly that she had not come in to see Lou today. But she couldn't retreat now.

"*You* love John," Lou said steadily. "Why don't you take him?"

"He hasn't asked me."

"You haven't let him. You've kept him away. Eleanor, it'll probably kill me if you do, but why don't you——"

"I can't!" The words were torn from Eleanor's throat. "It's true. I love him and I think he loves me, but—I can't marry him. It's as much as I can bear now. I think if I was married to him I'd go crazy. I'd die a little every time he went out of the house. Every time I heard a shot or saw someone running past my window I'd think it was him. I don't think I could stand it."

"He'd give it up," said Lou. "He doesn't like it any more than you do."

"He wouldn't give it up!" exclaimed Eleanor. "No more than the Reverend Fellows would give up the cloth and don a bartender's apron. I've seen it in John. Those first few weeks in Broken Lance. His eyes were dead all the time. He saw things happening here and knew that they shouldn't happen, that he should stop them. And he didn't. Now, he's doing it, and he's alive. He's in danger every minute of the day and night. He may be killed any hour—but he's *alive*."

Lou nodded slowly. "I believe you're right. I didn't think you'd noticed it. John feels he is destined for his task. He has the utmost confidence in himself. He knows he's doing the right thing. His job."

"I talked to him in the hospital last winter," said Eleanor. "I didn't know then why he was there and I couldn't understand him at all. He was so young and yet—so old."

Lou smiled wryly. "Well, it's pretty much a mix-up all around. Tom Waggoner loves me and I love John. John doesn't know I'm alive, because of you. And you won't take John because he's a law officer."

The revealing confidences had brought them closer together than they had ever been. Lou was jealous of Eleanor and wasn't ashamed to admit it. And Eleanor had bared her heart to Lou. They talked of the bazaar the next week and Lou promised to make a new hat for Eleanor.

It was three o'clock when Eleanor left the millinery shop. Since his escapade of the last visit to town, Mose had learned his lesson. He was in the buckboard when she approached it.

"I'm ready to go home now, Mose," she told the Negro. "Have you seen Mr. McSorley?"

Mose scratched his head. "He done went into Mr. Barat's saloon, 'bout a half hour ago. Hain't seen him since."

Eleanor didn't want to summon the foreman, but she

realized her uncle would be worried about her if she wasn't home for supper. So she said to Mose: "Run over to the saloon and tell him we're leaving. But he doesn't have to come yet if he doesn't want to. I just want him to know we've gone."

Mose ran across the street and entered Jeff Barat's main saloon. He came back two or three minutes later, scratching his head.

"I dunno, Miss Eleanor," he said. "Mistuh McSorley, he don't feel so good."

"He's drunk?"

"Well, I don't rightly know. But he's sittin' by a table and he's got his head on it and he don't seem to know what I was sayin'."

So he'd gone and gotten himself drunk. Eleanor was slightly annoyed, but then realized she couldn't blame poor McSorley. He hadn't wanted to go to the saloon. She'd practically forced him to go.

"All right, Mose," she said. "We'll go home alone."

"Yassum," exclaimed Mose. He untied the lines from the team of broncs and backed the wagon out to the middle of the street.

"Miss Simmons!" called Jeff Barat, from the sidewalk.

"Wait, Mose," Eleanor ordered.

Jeff Barat came out to the street and stopped with one boot on the hubcap of the buckboard. He doffed his black silk hat and showed his teeth in a wide smile.

"I've been looking for you, Eleanor," he said.

"Yes?"

"Yep. Town's havin' a church bazaar next week. Wanted to ask if you'd be my guest."

Eleanor was annoyed. She wished she could have got away without Barat seeing her.

"I'm sorry," she said. "But I haven't decided yet if I'd go."

"But if you do, you'll let me take you?"

"I'll let you know later," Eleanor replied evasively.

Jeff Barat's eyes glinted a little. But he backed away from the wagon.

"Fine, Eleanor, fine," he said.

Mose let out the broncs and they galloped down the dusty main street of Broken Lance. When they were out of town they slowed to a trot and kept that mile eating pace until they were halfway to the ranch of Ollie Simmons.

Then, from a small grove of cottonwoods rode three men: Deputy Sheriff Kelso and two men Eleanor had never seen before.

"Howdy, Miss Simmons," the deputy sheriff said.

Eleanor looked coolly at him.

"Good afternoon."

She nodded to Mose and he shook the lines. The horses started forward. Kelso's horse was in the way of the team and had to shy to one side.

"You damned dog!" Kelso exclaimed, angrily.

Mose winced.

"Sorry, boss!" he apologized.

"Sorry, hell!" snapped Kelso.

He whipped out a Frontier Model Colt and deliberately sent a bullet through Mose's head.

Eleanor screamed in horror. The dead body fell sidewards off the seat of the buckboard, struck a wheel and thudded to the sun-baked earth. The broncs, started by the shot, plunged forward.

Kelso and his riders yelled and clawed at the bridles of the horses. They clung to them and dragged the horses to a halt. Kelso meanwhile rode up beside the pitching buckboard and reached for Eleanor Simmons. She tried to evade him, but he leaned far from his horse's saddle. He caught hold of her arm and tore her cruelly from the buckboard. She fell to the ground and he let go of her.

Ollie Simmons had Emily hold the dinner until six-thirty. When she didn't show up then, he ate, but his appetite was small. When he finished eating he came out of the house and stood on the veranda, where he could look down the road that led to Broken Lance.

He knew that Jack McSorley had gone with Eleanor. He knew, too, how McSorley felt about his niece. He wasn't blind. She was safe, therefore. As long as Jack McSorley was alive.

Yet it wasn't like Eleanor to stay in town so late. He looked at his stem-winder and saw that it was ten minutes after seven. He sighed and muttered under his breath.

Russ Coe strolled from around the rear of the house.

"Eleanor get back from town?" he asked.

Ollie Simmons looked coolly at his hired gunfighter. "What business is it of yours?"

"Maybe none," said Russ Coe easily. "'Cept that Jack's been shinin' up to her. Maybe they eloped."

Ollie Simmons cursed roundly. "Russ, I've taken your pap once too often. Get your horse and clear off this ranch."

Russ Coe did not move. "You can't fire me, Ollie. On account of I already quit you. Yesterday."

Ollie Simmons' eyes became slits.

Russ Coe grinned. "I been workin' for Jeff Barat since yesterday."

"Get your horse!"

"In a minute. I'll get yours then, too. Because—Eleanor isn't coming home this evening."

Ollie Simmons made a swift move and a gun leaped into his hand. "Talk, Coe! Talk quick or I'll blow your head off!"

"That'd be the worst mistake you ever made in your life, Ollie," said Russ Coe easily. "If you killed me, Eleanor would *never* set foot on this ranch again."

"Where is she?" Simmons demanded thickly.

Coe looked down at his hands. "Some fellas have got her. They won't let her go unless I tell them."

Simmons actually trembled with the effort he made to keep from squeezing the trigger of the gun in his hand. "What do you want?"

Coe drew a sheet of folded paper from his pocket. "Like to have you write your name on this."

"What is it?"

"What diff'rence does it make? You sign it or you don't. If you don't you never see the girl again."

Through Simmons' mind ran the thought of what he would have done if this had happened to him two months ago. It was a repugnant thought. He slipped his Frontier Model .44 back into his holster.

"I'll sign."

"Good. Then I'll take you to the girl."

Eleanor Simmons sat in the home made chair and stared at Kelso, the deputy sheriff of Baker County.

"You know you can't get away with this," she said.

Kelso chuckled. "Mebbe not. Mebbe John Bonniwell will come and rescue you."

Eleanor's chin went up in the air. "Perhaps he will."

A bearded ruffian came into the room and said, "They're comin'."

"How many?"

"Just two. Coe an'——"

"Bonniwell?"

The ruffian cleared his throat. "Yep."

"All right, stay in here. Keep your mouth shut." Kelso went swiftly out of the room.

Ollie Simmons knew they were headed for Jeff Barat's ranch long before they came in sight of the buildings. He was surprised however, when he and Russ Coe approached, to recognize Kelso leaning against the door.

The door was closed.

Simmons dismounted.

"Where's my niece?" he demanded.

"Inside," replied Kelso. "You sign that paper?"

"He signed," said Russ Coe.

Kelso nodded and stepped away from the door. "All right, you can go in, Bonniwell!" He yelled the name. Russ Coe had compelled Simmons to take off his gunbelts before they'd left the ranch, but he hadn't noticed, when Simmons had put the pen and ink away, that the rancher had scooped a short-barreled derringer from a drawer and thrust it inside his shirt.

Now, the instant Kelso yelled, Simmons whirled, clawing at his shirt. It was a slow draw. Kelso's gun was out and thundering before Ollie Simmons cleared the derringer.

Simmons gasped and stumbled to his knees in front of the door. Kelso shot him again, through the chest. Simmons pitched silently forward on his face.

Russ Coe came forward. "The old——" he said. Then Ollie Simmons' hand lifted a couple of inches. The fingers contracted and the little derringer barked.

Coe screamed and clawed at his throat. For a horrible moment he swayed, then plunged to the earth, his head striking less than a foot from Ollie Simmons'.

His teeth parted in a snarl, Kelso stepped forward and placed his Frontier Model against Simmons' head. He pulled the trigger.

A moment later he entered the house. Eleanor Simmons was struggling in the embrace of the bearded ruffian.

"The hellion bit me!" the ruffian snarled.

"Let her go!" Kelso ordered.

Released, Eleanor stared wild-eyed at Kelso. "What've you done to him?"

"Him? You mean Bonniwell?" Kelso shook his head. "He got away, damn him."

He saw the relief that flooded Eleanor's face and said, brutally: "But your uncle and Russ Coe were just comin' up. Bonniwell killed them both.".

Eleanor's hand flew to her mouth, but could not quite suppress a scream.

"He's a hellion, that Bonniwell," said Kelso. "I'm gonna have to arrest him."

"I don't—believe you!" whispered Eleanor.

"You can go outside and look. And there're a couple of horses out there, too. You can climb up on one of 'em and go on home."

"What?"

Kelso scowled. "Say, what're you tryin' to make out—that I *kidnaped* you? Hell, Miss, I'm the deputy sheriff of this county. Your damn man pulled a gun on me and I killed him. You were afraid to go home, so I brought you over here. Then your uncle and Bonniwell came here and got into a fight. That's my story, and I got witnesses. You try to prove anythin' different!"

Kelso rode into Broken Lance and sought out Jeff Barat.

"McSorley still here?" he asked.

Barat showed his teeth. "He's drunk. Maybe he'll say he got knockout drops. He's a liar. You got the paper?"

"Yeah. And you know what—Russ Coe and Simmons killed each other!"

Muscles stood out on Jeff's jaws. "That's too bad. What are you going to do now?"

"I got witnesses to prove Bonniwell killed Ollie Simmons, outside of Broken Lance. I guess I'll have to arrest him. Uh, you got it fixed here?"

Barat chuckled. "Do you know, that fool Josh Hudkins believed all that stuff about Broken Lance being a city, and bought a heluva lot of stuff for his store. Even laid in a big line of farm implements. And he borrowed the money from our bank."

"That's fine, that's fine!"

Ten minutes later, Len Kelso, Mayor Josh Hudkins, and two of Kelso's cohorts called on John Bonniwell, in Tom Waggoner's office.

"Mr. Bonniwell," said Kelso. "Where were you between four and eight o'clock this evening?"

Bonniwell's eyes darted about the group. They lingered on the face of Josh Hudkins. The mayor of Broken Lance seemed agitated about something.

"I was sleeping in back here most of the time. Usually do from about three to six, because I work nights. Why?"

"Well, I think you rode out of town, down to Jeff Barat's ranch. You met Ollie Simmons there, with his man, Russ Coe. You had some words with him and—well, they're both dead."

"You lie, Kelso!" said Bonniwell.

"I saw you. So did these boys. We heard Simmons call you by name. So did Miss Eleanor!"

Bonniwell tensed. "Eleanor Simmons?"

"Yes. I met her on the road. Her boy'd gone wild and I had to shoot him. I was takin' her home when—when the rest happened."

"She said she saw me shoot her uncle?"

"She heard you and her uncle. I got a warrant here for your arrest."

Bonniwell took a quick step back.

"What is this?" he demanded.

"Judge Olcott issued the warrant," said Josh Hudkins, his lips twitching.

Bonniwell stared at him. "You've thrown in with them, Josh?"

Hudkins was silent for a moment. Then he half whispered, "No, but——"

"All right," said Bonniwell. "What do you want?"

"Yore guns, first," said Kelso. "Then we'll take a walk down to see the judge."

Bonniwell had never thought he'd surrender his guns to a Len Kelso. But he did now. There wasn't anything else he could do. Kelso was a deputy sheriff. He was backed by the county judge and the mayor of Broken Lance. And Bonniwell was himself an officer of the law.

Judge Olcott was in the courtroom in the chair that Judge Stone had formerly occupied. Bonniwell saw the little fat man and remembered how he had once saved his life. There was no gratitude in Olcott's face, though. Men who have been shown up as cowards seldom like brave men.

"This is a serious charge, Mr. Bonniwell," Olcott said.

"It's a frameup!"

Olcott shook his head. "These men swore out the complaint. All I can do now is remand you to the custody of the sheriff's office, for an early trial."

"Meaning——"

"That you go to jail," said Kelso.

Bonniwell sighed. He had put other men in the jail downstairs. He could stand a night in it, himself.

"Let's go," he said.

When Tom Waggoner came in from showing a prospective settler a half section of land south of Broken Lance, he learned what had happened. He went wild. He rushed down to the jail and was promptly headed off by Len Kelso, who was lounging outside the place.

"Prisoners can't talk to people outside!" he said curtly.

Waggoner swore at Kelso, then turned and dashed up the street to Josh Hudkins' store. The merchant was gray in the face.

"Wasn't anythin' I could do 'bout it," he said. "The warrant was legal."

"But they're murderers!" cried Waggoner. "You know damn well that Bonniwell never killed Eleanor Simmons' uncle. Russ Coe, perhaps, but not her uncle."

"The girl said he did."

"How do you know she said that? Did you hear her?"

"No, but they said she——"

"And you believed them in preference to Bonniwell." Waggoner's face blackened. "You've gone to the other side. You——" he choked and rushed out of the store.

At the livery stable he hired the best horse, mounted it and rode out of Broken Lance at a full gallop.

The animal was about ready to drop when he reached the Simmons' Ranch. There he found a score of sullen-eyed men congregated outside the main ranchhouse.

Waggoner walked past them and pounded on the door. Emily, the cook, her eyes red and swollen, came to the door.

Waggoner brushed past her. He found Eleanor in the newly furnished living room. She was sitting by the window, a handkerchief in her hand. But her eyes were dry.

"Eleanor," said Waggoner. "I know how you feel at a time like this and I'm sorry, but I must know—*did you see Bonniwell do it?*"

She shook her head. "No, but they called out his name."

"Did you hear *his* voice?"

She was silent for a moment and he saw her biting her lips. Then the word came, whispered: "No."

Waggoner strode out of the house.

Chapter Twelve

FINISH FIGHT

ON KANSAS STREET eighteen saloons were roaring full blast. Raw whisky was being tossed down throats, sore from whooping and yelling. Fiddles scraped and pianos tinkled and boots pounded the rough floors. Texas men were making up for lost time. Tomorrow or the day after they'd be riding down the Chisholm Trail, their pockets empty, their heads thick and befuddled.

And over on Church Street, the real citizens of Broken Lance were having a church bazaar. There was entertainment, too, but it was tame compared to that which could be had on Kansas Street.

There were women and children here. There were a half dozen unmarried ladies, too. Lou Sager was easily the most attractive of them. She was also the most popular woman at the bazaar, if the swarm of men that surrounded her was any criterion.

Tom Waggoner, coming late to the bazaar, had to wait ten minutes before he could get even a word with Lou. But finally, when practically every man present was rushing to buy the numbered paddles for the raffle of the gorgeous Spanish shawl, Waggoner caught Lou's arm.

"I've got to talk to you, Lou."

She searched his face and went quickly to a corner with him. "What's the trouble?"

"John. I've had a report that there's a plot to get him, tomorrow."

"Oh, Tom!" exclaimed Lou.

There was no mistake about it. The tension of her, the look on her face. It told Tom Waggoner. He would have given his soul if all that were for him.

But it wasn't. It was for John Bonniwell, Tom Waggoner's best friend.

"They won't let me to him," he said. "It's to be some time either before or during the trial. He ought to be warned."

"I can get to him," she said. "They won't forbid me to see him for a minute. I can wind that Kelso around my finger. I've seen it in his face."

"Yes," said Tom Waggoner. He looked at her and smiled a little. "You love him, Lou."

She started. "Who?"

"John, of course."

Her fine eyes came up and looked bravely into his. "Yes. But he's in love with Eleanor Simmons."

"And I'm in love with you. You know that?"

She nodded.

There was a scuffling of boots coming toward them. Men with paddles they'd bought for her. Waggoner said, "Tell him——"

Impulsively, she reached to take hold of his arm. But he was gone. Men were talking to her, pressing paddles on her. She managed to peer through the ring and saw Tom Waggoner stop at the door. She thought she caught his eyes for a moment, and then he was gone.

Waggoner walked down the south side of Kansas Street, with his hands in his pockets, his head slightly bent, studying the uneven sidewalk. And not seeing it.

He came to the Broken Lance Saloon and Dance Hall, Jeff Barat's headquarters, and looked at the rectangle of light that came through the window. He heard the dull roar of sound that came through the batwing doors. He went in.

The only law in Broken Lance tonight was Barat law. Texas men could do anything they liked, provided it didn't interfere with Mr. Jeff Barat's personal views. You could drink and curse, shout and gamble in Mr. Barat's saloon. You could shoot your guns into the floor or ceilings. Bullet holes didn't hurt much.

The only thing you couldn't do was cross the minions of Mr. Barat, who were here and there, on raised perches, the lookouts who protected Mr. Barat's interests. There was a big game going on tonight. Mr. Pearson of Texas had sold a herd of four thousand choice beeves to a Chicago buyer, at the very nice price of thirty-one dollars a head. It was a new high. Mr. Pearson had paid off all his cowboys. They were celebrating in their own way.

Mr. Pearson was playing poker. Naturally such a game

required the presence of Mr. Jeff Barat himself. To make it good, the deputy sheriff, Mr. Kelso, was sitting in. Also the leading banker of Broken Lance, Kansas, Mr. Ferdinand Barat.

The game was probably the largest that Broken Lance had ever seen. And big games were the rule in Broken Lance.

Tom Waggoner stopped at the table. Jeff Barat looked up at him.

"Mr. Waggoner," he said. "How come you're not at the church bazaar?"

"The games are too small. And too honest. I like them big and not so honest. Like this one."

"You talk too much, Waggoner!" snarled Len Kelso.

"Perhaps you'll shut my mouth some time, Mr. Kelso," retorted Waggoner.

"Maybe I will," said Kelso, half rising from his chair.

"Kelso!" exclaimed Jeff Barat. He looked up at Waggoner and a sneer twisted his mouth. "Why don't you get in the game, Mr. Waggoner, and keep it honest?"

One of Barat's men rose quickly from a chair and Waggoner sat down.

"I haven't much money with me," he said. "Is my credit good?"

"It is, Mr. Waggoner," offered Ferdinand Barat.

Cards came to Waggoner. Pearson, the drover, on Waggoner's right opened the pot. "Fifty dollars."

Waggoner's eyes slitted. It *was* a big game. Waggoner had a pair of fours. He called the bet. Ferdinand Barat, on his left, raised the opening amount by two hundred. Kelso dropped out. Waggoner had expected that. Jeff Barat, of course, stayed.

Pearson drew three cards and bet two hundred dollars. Waggoner looked at his three draw and discovered to his surprise that he had been given three tens, which gave him a full house. He called Pearson's bet, guessing that one of the other players would raise.

It went to Jeff Barat. He kicked it up five hundred dollars. Pearson called and raised it another five hundred. Ferd Barat dropped out. Waggoner merely stayed.

It was up to Jeff Barat now. He counted out one thousand dollars, pushed it into the pot, then played with a thick stack of bills for a moment and suddenly tossed it all to the center.

"And three thousand!"

Pearson licked his lips and studied his cards. He exhaled heavily and tapped the table, "I pass."

Waggoner looked coldly at Jeff Barat. "I drew three very good cards, Mr. Barat. I'd like to play them. How good is my credit?"

"Very good, Mr. Waggoner. You name the amount."

"All right, Mr. Barat—shall we say twenty thousand?"

The sardonic smile went from Jeff Barat's face. He looked at his brother, whose face remained impassive.

"You drew three cards?" he asked.

"You're the dealer, Mr. Barat."

A tiny glint came to Barat's eye. "All right, twenty thousand it is. And I call you. I drew only one card and it gave me five black spades."

"Which are not quite good enough," said Waggoner, steadily. He spread out his hand.

"Damn!" swore Len Kelso. "On a three card draw!"

"A very nice pot," said Ferdinand Barat.

It was. A fifty thousand dollar one. It made Broken Lance history. Jeff Barat sent a man for money. The game went on and Jeff Barat played savagely. Kelso borrowed a thousand dollars from Jeff Barat and lost it in ten minutes. He dropped out of the game.

That left the two Barats, the drover, Pearson, and Tom Waggoner. And Tom Waggoner, playing tonight with an indifference he had never possessed before, found Lady Luck perched on his shoulders. He won a ten thousand dollar pot, two or three smaller ones and then, with four kings against Jeff Barat's four jacks took the gambler for another thirty thousand dollars.

Jeff's face was white and taut. His brother's eyes were alarmed and he leaned over to whisper to Jeff. The latter listened for a moment and shook his head angrily.

"Got enough, Mr. Barat?" Waggoner taunted.

"My I.O.U. is good, isn't it?" snapped Jeff Barat.

Waggoner smiled thinly. It was his deal. He dealt the cards out deliberately and looked at his hand. It was a complete bust.

"I open for two thousand," Jeff Barat said savagely.

Pearson dropped out, followed by Ferdinand Barat.

"I'll stay with you, Mr. Barat," said Waggoner. He discarded two cards, retaining a jack, an eight and a five. It was the worst kind of poker, but Waggoner was no longer playing poker. He was playing himself against Jeff Barat.

Barat drew one card and looked at it only briefly. Waggoner believed he had two pairs, his openers. He looked at his draw, discovered that he'd given himself another five and a nine.

"Yes, Mr. Barat?"

Jeff scribbled on a slip of paper. "Five thousand!"

Waggoner smiled. He counted out five thousand dollars and continued. The others at the table watched him. When he got to twenty thousand Jim Malachy exclaimed softly. Waggoner glanced up, saw a fine film of perspiration on Jeff Barat's face and continued counting. He stopped when he reached fifty thousand.

Jeff Barat's eyes were bulging. His breath came hoarsely, from deep in his throat. His brother stared at him.

Slowly Jeff shook his head. "You win!"

Deliberately, Tom Waggoner flipped his cards face up. "I think I bluffed you that time, Mr. Barat!"

Jeff Barat's chair crashed over backwards as he leaped to his feet. "You——" he said.

Slowly, Tom Waggoner got to his feet. "I'm going to let that pass, Mr. Barat. I'm going to give you a real bet. I have eighty-five thousand dollars on this table. And here—" he stooped and quickly scribbled on a slip of paper—"is my I.O.U. for one hundred thousand dollars more. Mr. Barat, I'll cut you high card——"

"Don't do it, Jeff!" cried Ferdinand Barat in an agony of fear.

Jeff Barat was choking with rage. For years he had prided himself on being a gambler. And tonight this amateur had shown him up. Half the men in the saloon were listening now and watching. Barat had to accept whatever challenge Waggoner made. But a hundred and eighty-five thousand dollars—Jeff knew that he and his brother did not have that much money. If Waggoner should win—and the devil was riding with him tonight—they would have to give him half the real estate they owned in and around Broken Lance.

And while Jeff Barat was thinking it over, Waggoner said it all, in plain words. "——and I don't want you to put up one cent of money against this hundred and eighty-five thousand. I want you to do just one thing, instead—call off the killer you've got planted to get John Bonniwell tomorrow!"

Jeff Barat gasped. Then he did the only thing he could do. He whipped out his gun.

"Waggoner, you've gone too far!" he choked.

"I'll arrest him!" cried Kelso, the deputy sheriff. "He can't talk like that in public!"

Tom Waggoner sneered in Barat's face. "This is showdown, Barat. You can't kill me here. Not after the bet I've made." He jerked his head toward the saloon in general and Barat knew that Waggoner was right. The way Waggoner had put the proposition, eighty-five thousand dollars in actual money, plus a note for a hundred thousand, which everyone in Broken Lance knew was as good as money, removed the stigma of insult. No man insulted another with that much money.

It was direct challenge. Jeff Barat had to accept it, or be through in Broken Lance.

He fought for control, and when he won, put his gun back into its holster. "You're talkin' crazy, Waggoner, but I'll take you up. If you win, I'll take every one of my men and go with them personally to guard Bonniwell."

Waggoner shook his head. Barat swallowed hard and said: "My word he'll live through tomorrow."

"All right," said Waggoner. "They've heard that promise."

He stooped and riffled the deck of cards quickly, pushed them to Ferdinand Barat to cut. The banker's face was black. He cut the cards carefully.

Jeff Barat cut and showed the queen of hearts. A triumphant look began to spread on his face, and then Waggoner cut and turned up the king of spades. His luck had held to the end.

Murmurs of awe ran through the Texas men in the saloon. Waggoner's face relaxed. His eyes became bleak. He took off his hat and swept into it his winnings. Carelessly, he walked out of the saloon.

Jeff Barat sat down at the card table.

"Well," said Pearson, the drover. "Shall we resume?"

"After that?" exclaimed Ferdinand Barat. He got up, shook his head. "I think I'll go home."

After a moment, Jeff Barat caught Kelso's eyes and got up and went into his private office. Kelso came in a minute later. He sat down and waited for Barat to speak to him. Barat poured out a stiff drink from a bottle on his desk, then took a thin cigar from his pocket and lighted it. When he got it going good he had control of himself.

"There was a man in Montana once who bluffed me," he said. "He's dead now."

Kelso nodded. "Any particular way you want it?"

"Yes. He shot his mouth off. It's got to look right. And there's a damn good way to make it look right. He walked out of here with a hatful of money. A hundred thievin' Texans saw him go out. Would it be *our* fault if a couple of them should rob him———"

Kelso's face broke into a huge smile. "Say, that's great!"

"It's got to be perfect, Kelso! You can't just kill him and say a Texas man did it. You've got to *prove* it. Here's how. Waggoner's not going to give up his money without a fight. He kills one of the thieves—better make it two."

"You mean———"

Barat shook his head impatiently. "Of course not one of our boys. There are a dozen men out there who've spent their last half dollar. Get two of them. Tell them you'll split four ways with them and give them a free ticket down the trail. They'll go with you."

For a moment Kelso stared at his chief. Then he nodded slowly. "All right, Barat."

"Can you and Slingerland handle it?"

"Waggoner isn't Bonniwell. I'll take Cassidy along to make sure."

They left the Broken Lance Saloon and Dance Hall separately and met in the alley at the mouth of Texas Street.

"Got your horses, boys?" Kelso asked the two Texas men.

"All saddled," replied one of them.

"Fine. Here's the plan, then. He sleeps in a little room behind his office. You boys will tie your ropes on the back wall—it's only inch planking. When I give the signal, you pull. The whole back end will give way. The rest of us'll jump him, then."

"Why don't we do it the easy way?" one of the cowboys asked. "Just call him to the front door and buffalo him. Then we can go in and look for the money. He might have it cached."

"He has. He's got a tin box in there, chained to the wall. The back wall. That's why we ought to tear it down."

They agreed, of course, to Kelso's plan. But when they

got to the alley behind Waggoner's office, Kelso changed the plan.

"On second thought, you boys want your horses ready to roar the minute we get the money. Better if you, Slingerland and Cassidy, get your horses and do the pulling and the rebs help me with Waggoner."

In five minutes they were ready. Kelso remained in the shadows with the cowboys, while the others crept up to Waggoner's building and did what they had worked out with Kelso.

They came out of the shadows, carrying black ropes. They tiptoed to where their horses were in the darkness. After a couple of minutes a voice said cautiously: "Ready."

Kelso slipped his two Colts out of their holsters. He gestured to the Texas men. They drew their own guns, started toward the building. Kelso stepped behind them and put his guns to within three inches of each bobbing head. He pulled the triggers of both guns.

The roar of the guns was almost drowned by the terrific wrench and tearing of the rear wall of Waggoner's building.

The moon revealed Tom Waggoner, fully dressed, springing up from his cot, a gun in his hand. It also gave Kelso light enough to direct his fire. His gun crashed and Tom Waggoner tripped and plunged to his knees. Kelso fired again and again.

Then return fire came from the spot where Waggoner was lying. Kelso yelped and jumped backward. Waggoner's gun crashed again and Kelso pitched to his face. Back in the alley, Slingerland and Cassidy rushed their horses forward. Their guns began a deadly fire. Flame lanced toward the open end of the frame shack. Bullets whacked and thudded.

"He got Kelso!" cried Slingerland. He slid his horse to its haunches and bounded down from the saddle. He dropped to examine Kelso and a last bullet came from Tom Waggoner. Slingerland cried out and fell across Kelso.

Cassidy whirled his horse and dashed away.

The gun battle had been too prolonged and vicious not to arouse Broken Lance, which ordinarily paid no heed to an occasional shot. Someone ventured into the alley behind Waggoner's office. He stumbled over a body and ran away. He returned later with many men.

John Bonniwell slept through the night. Long ago he had

schooled himself to sleep through blizzards and blazing sun, with worry gnawing at his heart.

Broken Lance was quiet in the morning. He felt a strange tingling in his veins while he smoked a cigarette. And then Mike, the jailer, came to ask what he wanted for breakfast.

He avoided Bonniwell's eye and stood half turned away while he asked the question. Bonniwell was an observing man.

"What's up, Mike?" he asked.

Mike cleared his throat noisily. "You heard the shootin' during the night, maybe?"

A sudden chill swept over Bonniwell. "What happened?"

"Why, uh, yore friend Tom Waggoner won a lot of money playin' poker down at Barat's place. Some damn thieves tried to rob him——"

Bonniwell started at the jailer. "Tom—not Tom!" he said.

"The town's buzzin' this mornin'," Mike continued. "They ripped away the whole back end of his place. He got four of them. Uh—the dep'ty sheriff was one o' 'em. Can you imagine that!"

A strange light came to Bonniwell's eyes. He turned away from the jailer and sat down on his cot.

Mike looked at him and kept his mouth closed for a moment. Then he asked: "What'd you like for breakfast?"

When Bonniwell did not answer, Mike walked softly out of the room.

So they had got Waggoner. Tom Waggoner, the best friend he had ever had in his life. The biggest man in Broken Lance; a man who would have risen far above Broken Lance.

He was dead. His blood had gone to feed the thirsty soil of Kansas.

They told Lou Sager about it when she entered the restaurant for her breakfast.

The light went out of her eyes and she turned and walked out again. She walked to her little millinery shop, went in and locked the door behind her. She sat down in a wooden rocking chair and stared at the rows of hats.

"He didn't want to live," she whispered aloud. "I saw it in his eyes last night. He loved me and I didn't love him. The cleanest, finest man I'll ever know. He's gone!"

Jeff Barat, of course, heard it first. Cassidy galloped his

horse straight from the scene of the crime to the rear of the Broken Lance Saloon and Dance Hall.

He slipped into Jeff Barat's private office and found the gambler biting his finger nails.

Barat tried to show an indifferent face to Cassidy.

"Where's Kelso and Slingerland?" he demanded. "I heard the shooting."

"They're dead," said Cassidy. "The thing went wrong."

Jeff Barat sprang to his feet. "What happened? Waggoner didn't——"

"He's dead, all right. We gave him a pound of lead. But he got Kelso and Slingerland."

Quickly, Cassidy described the awful thing that had happened in the rear of Tom Waggoner's quarters.

When he finished Jeff Barat cursed roundly. "You blundering fools, you should've all been killed."

"I didn't see you riskin' your hide," retorted Cassidy angrily.

"I'm risking my hide right now," snapped Jeff Barat. "They'll say I was behind it when they find Kelso and Slingerland there. Here, you've got to leave. Fork your horse and ride as far south as you can."

He thrust a handful of bills at Cassidy. The latter took them and shook his head. "Not enough for what I went through."

Jeff Barat swore and his hand started for his gun. But Cassidy had been expecting that. He was a split second ahead of Barat. The gambler's hands came up.

"You saw me lose almost all the money I had last night," snarled Barat. "What more do you want?"

Cassidy sneered. Jeff Barat pulled open a drawer of his desk and with Cassidy watching closely snapped out a handful of bills.

Cssidy took them and went to the alley door. He slipped out. That was the last anyone in Broken Lance ever saw of him.

Jeff Barat bolted the alley door, took a shotgun from a rack and saw that both barrels were loaded. He laid it on his desk, lit a thin cigar and dropped into his chair.

He was sitting there with the stub of the cigar in his mouth when Ferdinand came in some time later.

"You fool!" Ferdinand said coldly. "You've got the whole

town roused. They say you sent Kelso and Slingerland to kill him."

"I don't care what they say," retorted Jeff Barat. "They haven't got a leader. They're afraid to do anything about it."

"They'll have a leader in the morning!" snapped Ferdinand. "That man Bonniwell. Don't you see—Kelso's dead. He was the chief witness against Bonniwell. The judge'll dismiss the charge."

The stub of the cigar fell from Jeff Barat's lips. His jaws went slack.

Ferdinand regarded him in disgust. "You've gone all to pieces since last night. We're not licked yet, but from now on I'm running things."

"You're going to try to stick it out?"

"We've got to. Do you think I'll run from a cheap, claptrap little town like this without a profit?"

"You've got a plan?"

"Of course I have. I always have. I've already told a half dozen people outside that you fired Kelso and Slingerland last night. I hinted one of the reasons was because they'd thrown in with some thieving Texas men."

"How'd they swallow it?"

"Not so good. But I'll hammer it home. There're too many other things happening around here to keep their thoughts very long on one thing. If you lay low for three or four days we can bluff it out. I'm sure of that."

"Where'll I stay?"

"The ranch. You've got a small army of men there. Keep them close to the ranch and you're safe. I'll run things here and keep in touch with you."

At eight o'clock Judge Stone and Mayor Hudkins came to see Bonniwell.

"The witness against you is dead," said the justice. "No need your appearing in court."

Bonniwell got up from the cot on which he had been sitting for two solid hours.

"What are you going to do?" asked Josh Hudkins.

Bonniwell went to the door and said to Mike, the jailer. "My guns, Mike!"

Mike got them promptly. Bonniwell buckled them about his waist. He started for the door.

Hudkins ran after and caught him by the shoulder. "John, I know I sold you out. I couldn't help it. I was forced to do it. But to hell with the Barats. I'm with you again."

Bonniwell looked bleakly at him.

"Hudkins," he said, "I don't trust men who've backed down once. But I need something from you. I need the job of marshal of Broken Lance."

"Of course, John. I meant——"

Bonniwell walked out of the jail. Men were standing on the sidewalks in small clumps. They scattered, or were silent, when Bonniwell walked by.

He passed Lou Sager's shop and his jaws tightened. He did not look into the window. If he had, he would have seen Lou still sitting in the rocking chair, staring blindly at her shelves.

Somehow the front door of Waggoner's office was still locked. No one had thought to open it. Bonniwell left it locked and walked around the corner. When he got to the alley behind the flimsy building a half dozen morbid sightseers scattered before him. He waited until they had all gone.

Then he moved forward. He picked up an end of a cut rawhide riata and looked at it. It was easy enough to figure out how they had ripped the back of the building away. It had been built of flimsy lumber. You could have kicked the boards away from the inside.

The bodies, of course, were gone. But there were congealed pools and spots of dark colored stuff. Bonniwell examined them all. Slowly he reconstructed a story. After a half hour he left the alley.

Out on the street Judge Stone stopped him.

"Mr. Bonniwell," he said. "I've got Mr. Waggoner's things at my office. There's quite a lot of money, and some notes——"

"I wasn't his partner," said Bonniwell. "It'll have to be sent to his relatives. He's got a cousin or uncle somewhere in the East."

"We found some addresses in his effects," said the judge. "But, Mr. Bonniwell, we found something else, too. A will, made out by myself only a week ago. He left everything he owned to you!"

Chapter Thirteen

SHOWDOWN

BROKEN LANCE HAD EXPECTED THINGS of Bonniwell. He had been framed and publicly humiliated. He had been thrown in jail and while he was there, his best friend had been murdered.

Broken Lance knew John Bonniwell and it expected him to do something about things.

He disappointed Broken Lance. He did nothing. After his examination of the alley behind Waggoner's office, he went straight to the county jail and slumped into the swivel chair behind his desk. He stayed there all day, not even going out to eat lunch. One or two citizens ventured to come in during the day, but when he looked at them, they mumbled an apology and quickly retreated.

Broken Lance was very quiet that day. It was counting its broken bones and licking its wounds. Bonniwell was the key man to everything—and he did nothing.

At five-thirty Bonniwell finally left the marshal's office. With slow, deliberate step he walked to Lou Sager's millinery shop. The door was locked and he started to turn away, but Lou Sager saw him through the window and came and opened the door. He went inside.

Lou was dry-eyed. She moved like an automaton.

"Broken Lance licked us," he said.

She nodded. "We'll miss him more than anyone else. We loved him."

"*You* loved him, Lou?"

"Yes," she replied simply. "I loved him and I didn't know it until today. Yesterday he asked me to marry him. I told him I was in love with you."

His eyes bored into hers, but he did not speak. She smiled wanly. "Today I know it was Tom. He was good."

"The best man I've ever known," said Bonniwell. "A far better man than I."

"He would be alive today, if I hadn't been so brutal to

him. I saw it in his eyes when he went away from me. He wanted to die."

Jack McSorley came in.

"Miss Simmons is outside," he said. "She sent me to see if it's all right——"

"Of course," said Lou.

Bonniwell cleared his throat awkwardly. "I—think I'd better go."

"Please stay here!"

Jack McSorley slipped out and Eleanor Simmons came in. She went straight to Lou and they embraced. There were no words they could say to each other. Each had lost a loved one.

Bonniwell would rather have faced a spitting gun than this situation.

The girls stepped away, and then Eleanor turned and looked at Bonniwell.

"He was a friend to be proud of," she said.

Lou Sager had two living rooms in the rear of her shop.

"I'm going in back," she said. "I'll give you five minutes."

Bonniwell saw the flush sweep from Eleanor's throat to her face. His own pulses suddenly pounded.

Lou walked firmly to the rear of the store, and Bonniwell felt like a schoolboy being called upon to recite before a classroom full of girls.

Eleanor's long lashes completely covered her eyes. She would not raise them. They were quiet until Bonniwell could stand it no longer.

"Eleanor!" he blurted. "You must know how I feel about you."

At last she raised her eyes.

"Yes, John," she said. "I know."

Bonniwell knew very well that he didn't move. He would have sworn, too, that Eleanor hadn't stirred an inch. Yet suddenly she was in his arms. Her face was buried in his shoulder and he thought she was sobbing.

And then her arms were up around his neck. He released her a little and her face turned up to his own. Their lips met in their first kiss.

Presently, though, she disengaged herself. Her face was scarlet, but her eyes looked honestly into his.

"I knew in St. Louis," he said.

"So did I. And—I thought I'd lost you."

"You know why I let you go?"

The shine in her eye dimmed a little. He saw it and said quickly: "It doesn't make any difference?"

"No," she said, but he knew it did.

Yet Bonniwell knew himself. Some men go all through life too busy to ever take time to understand themselves. Not Bonniwell. He was by instinct a lonesome and thoughtful man. He had gotten to know himself.

He said: "This is life. It's you and I and the people like Tom and Lou who'll make this country. Every one of us is necessary. Someone must plow the earth so you and I can eat. I must make it possible for someone to plow. It's my job. The only one I can handle."

She shook her head sadly. "You no longer have to argue with me about it, John. I've thought of it, hour after hour, day after day. I know it's so, but it doesn't make it any easier."

"I know," he conceded. "There's probably no one in all the world who's gotten less out of life, or who's hated it more. Don't you know I was sick for days before I met Doug Sutherland? And afterwards, but I had to get him. There wasn't any one else."

"Did he *have* to be killed?"

"Of course. It's the law of our civilization. The mad dog must be exterminated. Jeff Barat killed your uncle and Tom Waggoner. He must pay for that."

She took two full steps away from him. "You're still going to kill him, even after—this?"

Miserably, he shook his head back and forth. "I've got to. I couldn't live with myself if I didn't."

"But you can't, John. I won't let you. I've just found you now, and I won't take the slightest chance of losing you."

"I've got to do it, Eleanor. It's my duty."

"Before everything else?"

He loved her more than anything in the world, yet he turned away from her and stumbled to the door. As he opened the door, Lou came out of her living quarters in the rear and called to him.

"John, wait!"

But he went out. On the sidewalk, leaning against the hitching rail, was Jack McSorley. He fell in beside Bonniwell and walked with him for a hundred feet. Then he said: "You going to get Barat, John?"

"Yes," Bonniwell replied shortly.

"I should have got Kelso yesterday," said McSorley. "I promised myself I would. I waited too long."

Impatiently, Bonniwell left McSorley. He crossed the street to the Golden Prairie Saloon.

"I want to rent a room for a while," he told Sheidler, the proprietor.

"Number three, at the right end of the hall," Sheidler said. There was no key. Bonniwell went up to the room and stayed there until it was dark.

Then he came down and had supper at the restaurant across the street. Finished, he lit a cigar and walked across to the Broken Lance Saloon and Dance Hall. He found Jack McSorley at the end of the bar, with a bottle before him.

He walked up to him.

"Sorry, Jack," he said.

"S'all right. You got things on your mind. I know. Have a drink?"

Bonniwell shook his head. "Didn't you take Miss Simmons home, Jack?"

"She's stayin' with the girl in the hat shop. Don't blame her. Ollie gets buried tomorrow, and I'm gettin' drunk tonight." His face twisted tragically. "He changed when the girl came. I don't give a damn what they used to say about him—he was all man."

"He was, Jack."

McSorley poured another drink. "Couple free-state militiamen were going to hang me. Ollie saved my life. And I couldn't do a thing for him."

Bonniwell clapped him on the shoulder and turned away.

Ferdinand Barat, for some reason, was occupying the raised lookout's platform. He had a silk hat on his head and he was watching Bonniwell quietly.

Bonniwell walked over. "Jeff's at the ranch?"

Not a muscle moved in Ferd Barat's face. Bonniwell knew that what he'd always suspected was true, that Ferd Barat was by far the more formidable of the two brothers.

"You know, of course, that I'm going to get you both," Bonniwell said.

"We've still got a few cards," Barat finally said. He got up from his raised chair and stepped down to the floor level. "You're wrong, Mr. Bonniwell," he said. "I give you my word that you are. Jeff had nothing to do with what happened."

"Your *word*, Mr. Barat?"

Muscle rippled along the Wall Street man's big jaws. "My word." His word wasn't worth a Confederate paper dollar and Bonniwell knew it. He went to the bar, at the opposite end from Jack McSorley, and ordered a beer. He sipped at it slowly while he examined the idea that had popped into his mind while talking with Ferdinand Barat. He turned it over and looked at it from all sides and finally he nodded.

He walked out of the saloon and crossed the street to Lou Sager's shop. It was dark, but when he pressed his face to the window he saw a thread of light shining under the door between the store and the living quarters.

He knocked on the door and waited. After a while a rectangle of light appeared in the back, and after a moment, Lou's face was pressed to the window.

"It's me, Bonniwell!"

She unlatched the door and pulled it open. He saw that she had a long-barreled Frontier Model Colt in her hand and gave her a sharp look.

"Is Eleanor here?" he asked. "I must talk to her."

Lou stepped aside and let him into the store. She locked the door and followed him to the rear. When he stepped into a lighted living room at the rear, Eleanor exclaimed.

"I'm sorry," he said. "I had to talk to you about your uncle's affairs. Do you know in what condition they are?"

She looked at him strangely; then she shook her head. "No. There's a lot of cattle out there and I know he had money in the bank."

"That may be it. I've been trying to figure out why the Barats killed him. If he was dead, they couldn't expect to take over his ranch, unless— No, that isn't——"

"What?"

He bit his lip. "Jeff and you."

"I refused him two weeks ago. I made it sufficiently clear, I think."

"Then they had some other scheme."

Lou had come into the room and Bonniwell turned to include her. "Judge Stone told me this morning that Tom made a will a while ago, leaving everything to me."

"You were his best friend," said Lou, steadily.

"I don't want it, of course," said Bonniwell. "But I think I can beat the Barats with it. I don't imagine Ferdinand Barat had more than a couple of hundred thousand dollars when he came here. He spent it pretty recklessly for a while. I remember his bank statement said only $100,000 capital. He's bought up a lot of Tom's leases, paying big prices, and he's made loans on pieces of property he figured he'd get later on. He must be pretty near the bottom of the bin.

"Eleanor, will you work with me? Will you go in the first thing tomorrow morning and find out what your uncle had on deposit at the bank? If it's a very large amount I want you to draw it out. Insist on getting the money. There are some notes in Tom's effects that Jeff gave him. I'm going to force payment tomorrow."

"You think you can break the bank?" Eleanor asked.

Bonniwell nodded. "I've an idea. Without money the Barats are no more powerful than any two cowboys in this town. Less, even. A cowboy can live without money. They can't."

"Very well, John. I'll do as you say."

He flashed her a wan smile. "Thanks. Good night."

Bonniwell sat in front of the Golden Prairie Saloon the next morning when Eleanor Simmons went to the bank. She was inside no more than five minutes before she came out and returned to Lou Sager's shop. Bonniwell waited ten minutes, then got up and walked carelessly toward the courthouse and jail. He went inside for a few minutes, then came out and walked back up the street on the side of Lou Sager's shop.

He passed the place a few feet, then, as if struck by an afterthought, returned and went into the store. The girls were relieved to see him.

"John!" exclaimed Lou. "Eleanor just learned something shocking. Ferdinand Barat holds a mortgage on the ranch."

Bonniwell smiled grimly. "How much?"

"Thirty thousand dollars," said Eleanor. "And he—he said the bank would have to call it."

"And there's no money on deposit?"

"Just a few hundred dollars."

"You saw the mortgage? Did you notice when it was dated?"

"July 16th of this year."

"July 16th was one week after the bank started. I don't

believe it," said Bonniwell. "Your uncle was pretty sore at the Barats at the time. Anyway, why would he mortgage the ranch?"

"He had a heavy payroll."

"But he had plenty of stock. How many head, by the way?"

"Something like twenty thousand."

Bonniwell whistled. "Will you trust me, Eleanor—give me your power of attorney to act for you?"

"Of course."

Bonniwell went to the courthouse and spoke for several minutes to Judge Stone, after which the justice put on his hat and went out. He returned in ten minutes and handed a sheet of paper to Bonniwell.

A half hour later, Bonniwell walked into the Broken Lance Hotel, which was a part of Barat's Broken Lance Saloon & Dance Hall. A florid, middle-aged man with a huge gold watch chain strung across his paunch was reading a Kansas City newspaper.

Bonniwell sat down beside him.

"Mr. Colby, would you be interested in five thousand beeves?" he asked quietly.

The newspaper dropped from the cattle buyer's hands. "Who's got them to sell?"

"I have."

"You? Uh—ain't you Mr. Bonniwell, the town marshal?"

"Yes. But I have power of attorney from Eleanor Simmons, who owns these five thousand beeves. They're right here near Broken Lance and we can start delivery tomorrow."

"The market's down this week," Colby said cautiously.

"What's your price?"

Colby scowled. This was being thrust at him too unexpectedly. "Uh—twenty-one, no-no, nineteen dollars a head. Straight through."

"Your price is too low," said Bonniwell. "But we'll accept it, if you can pay for them right now."

"Now? What do you mean?"

"Within an hour."

Colby cleared his throat. "It's a deal. Most of the drovers insist on cash on the line, and I've got it, right across the street in Barat's bank. One hour it'll be."

"Do me a small favor. Don't go to the bank for a half hour."

"Eh? Why not?"

Bonniwell smiled disarmingly. "You know bankers. They're all Shylocks at heart. Friend of mine wants to play a trick on him."

The buyer laughed. "This Barat don't like jokes, they tell me."

"That's why it'll be funny."

Bonniwell went back to the courthouse. When he came out he carried a small bundle wrapped in a piece of paper. He carried it to Lou Sager's store and handed it to Eleanor.

"Take this to the bank and pay off the mortgage on the ranch," he said.

Her eyes widened and she shoved the package back at him. "I can't take——" she began, but he cut her off.

"I'm playing the last hand with Barat. The mortgage is a forgery, of course. Your uncle was killed, so Barat could make the mortgage stick and take over your ranch. He made a slip. He didn't make it big enough. Go down right now and bring the paper back with you."

Eleanor looked appealingly at Lou Sager, who nodded. When Eleanor had left the store, Lou said to Bonniwell: "I think you'll lose her if you kill again."

"I know," said Bonniwell. "There's been too much. But I think I've got Ferd Barat."

Eleanor returned, her face flushed angrily. "He didn't want to take the money. I had to threaten to go to Judge Stone. Here's the mortgage."

Bonniwell's eyes lit up in triumph. "I've got him."

He left the shop and walked directly to the bank. Ferdinand Barat's face was still red from his encounter with Eleanor.

"Well?" he snapped at Bonniwell.

Bonniwell laid several slips of paper on the desk.

"Like to cash in this paper of Jeff's," he said softly.

Barat stared at the notes. "Where'd you get those?"

"Here's a slip of paper from Judge Stone, stating that Tom Waggoner made me his sole heir. So I'm collecting on these—sixty-five thousand dollars!"

Ferd Barat's underjaw was slack. "Those are Jeff's, not mine."

"It says 'Brothers' on the window."

"All right," snapped Ferd Barat. "What of it? Jeff'll pay those sometime. I haven't got time to go into——"

"You've got time. You'll pay me sixty-five thousand dollars right now!"

"Those are gambling debts. They're not legal."

"In Broken Lance, Kansas, they are," said Bonniwell. "No one welches on a gambling debt out here. It's not healthy."

"You're threatening me?"

Bonniwell shook his head. "No. If you refuse to pay these notes I'm not going to press it. All I'll do is tack these pieces of paper up inside the Golden Prairie Saloon."

Ferd Barat licked his lips.

"All right," he said savagely. "I'll pay."

He went off and brought back a thick stack of bills, plus a smaller one. Bonniwell knew the thick stack was the one that Eleanor Simmons had brought in a few minutes ago.

When Bonniwell came out of the bank, it was just a half hour since he'd talked to Colby, the cattle buyer, and Colby was coming across the street. Bonniwell nodded as they passed in the middle of the street.

A few minutes later Colby came out of the bank.

Bonniwell's mouth twisted into a sardonic smile. Colby stopped three men before he came across the street. Every one of the men immediately dashed off, two of them to the bank. By the time Colby reached Bonniwell, there was a small stampede in the direction of the bank. Bonniwell didn't need Colby's words to tell him what was happening, but he listened, anyway:

"The bank's broke. Barat hasn't got ten thousand dollars in it!" Colby cried. "That's a heluva business."

"Shucks," said Bonniwell, easily. "Barat's got a lot of holdings. He's just temporarily hard up. He can realize a half million on his property."

"Can he?" cried Colby. "Who's got that much money?"

Bonniwell shrugged. "The deal's off, then?"

Colby groaned. "I dunno if the main office can raise that much money."

"Tell you what," said Bonniwell. "You make the price $21.00 a head and I'll take your order on the bank, in payment."

"*This* bank?"

"Yeah, sure. I got confidence in Broken Lance."

Colby caught hold of Bonniwell's arm and rushed him into the hotel. Bonniwell came out inside of three minutes and again took his customary seat.

There were a hundred men jammed about the entrance to the bank. More were converging upon it from all sides. Bonniwell saw one of the bank clerks rush out of a side street and scoot for the Broken Lance Hotel & Saloon. To get all the available cash, no doubt.

But the clerk didn't stop there. When he came out he rushed up the street to The Texan Bar.

Bonniwell smoked a long cigar down to less than two inches before Ferdinand Barat pushed his way through a howling mob in front of the bank. Most of the mob followed him across the street.

Barat was disheveled. His forehead was bathed in perspiration and there was a wild look in his eye.

"Bonniwell!" he cried, when he was a dozen feet away. "You've got all the ready cash in Broken Lance. I need it. Those fools think I'm broke and want their money, today. They won't believe I can get a million dollars from New York in three days."

Bonniwell put the stub of the cigar in his mouth and took a couple of quick puffs. "New York's a long ways from here. What security have you got here?"

"Half the property in this town. I'll give you a thirty-day mortgage on the whole works."

"No," said Bonniwell. "I knew a person once who got stung with a forged mortgage."

Ferdinand Barat showed his teeth in a snarl. He turned toward his frantic depositors. "He's got a personal grudge against me. He won't loan me the money under any circumstances."

The roar that went up in the street could have been heard two miles away. When it quieted down somewhat, Bonniwell said loudly: "I will loan the money, on certain conditions."

"What conditions?" grated Ferdinand Barat.

"Outright sale, no mortgages."

Barat staggered back. "Everything?"

"Uh-huh. I'll let you keep the bank. But everything else I take."

It was a bitter bargain for Barat. He swore and fumed, but the depositors behind him were threatening. He knew that he could not refuse to pay them their money and live. He ended by signing over everything to John Bonniwell. Everything but the bank.

At two-thirty in the afternoon the run on the bank stopped.

Everyone who'd had money in the bank and was in Broken Lance had drawn it out. Then Bonniwell strolled over to see Ferd Barat. He found the banker with a bottle of liquor on his desk, rapidly getting drunk.

"I'll never forget what you did to me, Bonniwell," he said coldly.

"Things I haven't forgotten, either," said Bonniwell. "You got any money left over, now that the run's stopped?"

"Forty thousand dollars, if it's any satisfaction to you."

"It's not enough. I've got a letter on you for one hundred and five thousand, written by Colby, the cattle buyer."

Ferdinand Barat knocked the whisky bottle from his desk and jerked open a drawer. With his hand on a gun, he looked at Bonniwell—and saw the Frontier model already thrown down on him.

"You're through, Barat!" Bonniwell said coldly. "Get your hat and get out. And if you're smart you'll keep right on goin' when you hit the street."

Barat didn't pick up his high silk hat. He went out, bareheaded. Bonniwell spoke to the clerks in the bank.

"Mr. Colby's given me a draft on this bank for one hundred and five thousand dollars," he said. "There isn't that much here, so I'm takin' the bank. Any objections?"

"Mr. Barat didn't make any," said one of the clerks.

"All right, then. Lock what money there is in the safe, then put the padlock on the door. The bank's closed."

Ferdinand Barat got a horse and buckboard from the livery stable and kept the animal at a solid run all the way to the ranch where Jeff was making his stand. But as fast as he traveled, Jeff already knew—about the run on the bank.

His eyes were like coals as he listened to his brother's account of the final crushing blow.

"We're finished, then?" he asked when Ferdinand concluded.

"I've got a hundred dollars in my pocket. All the money I've got in the world. I closed out everything in New York. You said we'd make millions out here in Kansas."

"I've got one more card to turn over," said Jeff Barat. "An ace."

He went to the door of the house and called to a man hunkered on his heels a short distance away. "Lafe, get every man in the saddle."

Ten men, including Lafe, showed up in the ranchyard a

few minutes later. Jeff Barat looked them over. "Where're the rest of the boys?"

"That's all, boss," said Lafe. "The others figured you were through. They beat it."

Jeff Barat cursed roundly. He walked to one of the horses. "Come on, Ferd!"

Ferdinand's broad forehead was creased into deep wrinkles. "What are you going to do?"

"What we should have done in the first place. Take over Broken Lance."

"What!"

"Most of the Texas men will throw in on our side when the showdown comes. Anyway, the town'll be disorganized. We'll get Bonniwell first of all. We'll *take* back what we lost."

"You can't, Jeff!" cried Ferdinand. "You can't fight that way!"

"The hell I can't. It's all I can do. Come on, boys!"

They left Ferdinand Barat. He watched them trot out of sight; then he climbed into the buckboard. He turned his horse due south. He knew when the game was lost. He was broke, poor, the first time in many years. He was heading down into a vast wilderness of which he knew nothing. Without a gun. With just a horse and buckboard—and a hundred dollars.

He didn't know that there wasn't a single store between him and Austin, Texas. He was a greenhorn from Wall Street, New York. His knowledge of high finance would not be of practical use to him when he encountered a band of Comanches, or Choctaws, or Creeks. A Texas cowboy could have made the trip with only a horse and a gun. Barat couldn't make it with a million dollars. And he had only a hundred.

Tears were in the eyes of both Lou Sager and Eleanor Simmons when Bonniwell told them of the coup. "Tom Waggoner made it possible," he said. "He did more in one evening than I could have done in a year."

"They've gone away now—the Barats?" asked Eleanor Simmons.

"Broke, Ferdinand Barat is nothing. Jeff, without his brother's backing, is no more than a gun-slingin' Texas man. It's all yours, Eleanor. Here——" He tossed papers into her lap. "You own Broken Lance, lock, stock and barrel."

"But what would I do with it?" she cried, bewildered. "I don't want it. Half of it was Tom Waggoner's."

"If you don't want Broken Lance," suggested Bonniwell, "keep your uncle's ranch and give the town to those to whom it belongs—the citizens of Broken Lance."

"Of course!" she exclaimed. "But you—you handle it."

"If you wish . . ." His eyes went to the window of the store. He saw the cavalcade riding past and his nostrils flared, Eleanor looked past him and inhaled sharply.

"Jeff Barat!"

"I didn't think he had the nerve," Bonniwell said. His hands dropped to his sides and he smiled at Eleanor, but it was an empty smile.

"No!" she cried. "No, John!"

"I'm still the marshal of Broken Lance."

"I don't care," she sobbed. "You've done enough. You've risked your life too many times. You can't win always."

"Maybe it's in the cards once more."

She made a helpless gesture. "Not for me, it isn't. If you go out there now, John, I'll never——"

A gun roared outside. Then another and another.

"I'm through," Eleanor said. "It's all gone in me."

"I'm sorry," he said, "but it's my job."

The yell of a dozen men rolled over Broken Lance. Guns thundered.

Bonniwell ran to the door of the millinery shop. He opened the door and leaped out to the street. The rear of Jeff Barat's forces were just storming into the Golden Prairie Saloon.

He cut diagonally across the street. Only one shot was fired inside the saloon, while he walked. But when he got to within fifty feet of it he could hear Jeff Barat's raucous voice.

He quickened his step, hurdled the sidewalk and put his shoulder against the batwing doors. He went through with his hands at his sides.

"All right, Barat!" he said.

Jeff Barat was by the bar. There was a gun in each of his hands. The muzzles were slightly depressed, but he was facing directly toward the door. He had only to tilt up the guns and squeeze the triggers.

"Right into the trap, Bonniwell!" he yelped.

Eight of Jeff Barat's followers were spread out fanwise, facing the door. The other two were caught behind the bar, near the till. Jeff Barat had come to open holdup and robbery. There were others in the saloon, twenty or thirty men. But they were at the tables. Most of them were Texas men. It wasn't their fight. If they were drawn into it, they'd as soon side with Barat. He, at least, was against organized law.

Jack McSorley sat at a table, closest to the bar. He had a half empty glass of whisky in his hand, and there was a bottle on the table before him. Bonniwell had a quick glimpse of the foreman of the Simmons Ranch and guessed that he had been at it ever since the night before, with little if any sleep. He was in bad shape.

Jeff Barat snarled: "You're not handlin' my brother now. It's me, Jeff Barat, you're up against." Slowly, imperceptibly, the muzzles of his Frontier Models crept up.

He was going to shoot without any warning at all. Bonniwell knew that. He wasn't going to give him any chances.

Bonniwell said: "Even if you shoot me first, I'll live long enough to kill you."

"You will like——" began Barat.

And then Jack McSorley let his glass of whisky slip from his hand and crash to the floor. He followed the glass. In the infinitesimal fraction of a second that Bonniwell took to glance at the falling foreman he saw the eyes of the man bright with purpose, saw his hand sneaking for his gun. Bonniwell knew then that McSorley wasn't as drunk as he had been pretending. That he was making his last play—avenging Ollie Simmons.

Barat was distracted by the breaking glass, by the catapulting of McSorley's body. His guns swiveled involuntarily; one of them roared. Frantically, then, he was throwing the guns back toward John Bonniwell. And it was too late. The Frontier Models were already in Bonniwell's hand. The right hand gun roared and Jeff Barat jerked.

The bullet didn't kill Barat quickly enough, but it spoiled his aim. He was only able to shoot Bonniwell in the left thigh.

The Golden Prairie Saloon exploded to a crescendo of gunfire. Guns thundered and boomed. Men screamed and yelled and rushed about. There were too many men shooting at too close range. There could be no accuracy.

Bonniwell knew only that he was alone, that all men were against him. He was down on one knee because of Jeff

Barat's bullet in his thigh. He fired methodically and with aim.

Red fire seared his ribs; an invisible fist smashed him high on the right side of the chest, bowled him over backwards into the rough hewn bar. He came out of that, propped on his right elbow, his left hand gun ready to fire.

But there was no one at whom to shoot. There were still men in the saloon, but they were crouched behind overturned tables and chairs, seeking to dodge flying bullets rather than to throw them. A veritable hush hung over the interior of the saloon.

A crooked smile played over John Bonniwell's lips.

He heard galloping horses outside, then the pound of many hurrying boots. Josh Hudkins, Jake Sheidler and a half dozen men, rifles, shotguns and revolvers in their hands, swarmed into the saloon.

"Bonniwell!" cried Josh Hudkins.

Bonniwell let his gun clatter to the floor.

"From now," he said, "you can hire a policeman with a stick to patrol Broken Lance."

And then he fainted.

From the cot that had been arranged for him next to the window, Bonniwell could look over Broken Lance. It annoyed him that he could scarcely move. His left leg was in rigid splints, his waist was tightly taped and his right shoulder so wrapped in bandages he could only wiggle fingers of that hand.

But by twisting his head, he was able to see Kansas Street. Strangely, a farmer's wagon, standing in front of the Golden Prairie Saloon, caught his eye. A gleaming plowshare stuck out over the tailboard. A little boy of seven or eight was sitting on it. There were, in the wagon, four or five other children. And a woman with a huge sunbonnet.

There was a footstep on the left of him and he rolled his head back. Eleanor Simmons looked down on him, her face as he had seen it only once before.

She was wearing a green velvet traveling costume.

Bonniwell's nostrils flared a little. "You're going——"

"Not going," she shook her head. "I'm coming—with you."

"All the way to St. Louis?"

"To that very same hospital. But you're not going to stay there as long as you did the last time!"

He was an understanding man. He didn't require even the pressure of her soft warm hand over his own, to know. But he liked it. He liked, too, the lips that came down to meet his own.

Bantam Books is proud to present
a Special Preview of the winner of the
Bantam Books/Twentieth Century-Fox
First Western Novel Contest

SEASON OF VENGEANCE
by W. W. Southard

Coming in April, 1981

© Copyright 1981, W.W. Southard

The Bantam Books/Twentieth Century-Fox First Western Novel Contest, conducted in 1980 was designed to encourage previously unpublished novelists in the writing of the kind of quality Western fiction that has entertained readers and moviegoers for decades. W.W. Southard's SEASON OF VENGEANCE was selected as the winning novel from approximately 1,000 manuscripts that were submitted to the contest.

Mr. Southard is a native of New Mexico and he says of his first Western, "I have tried to give readers a picture of the men and women who tamed the frontier, and of those who died trying."

We hope you enjoy this specially selected preview section of SEASON OF VENGEANCE.

In the doorway of the little adobe house, Jessie Ramming kissed Anna long and hungrily and held her against him in a gentle, careful embrace. Then he swung into the saddle and reined his gray horse away, past the shed and the pole corral, toward the dry creek bed beyond.

He looked back once and saw her still standing there shading her hazel eyes against the early sun. Jessie had to smile. If she lived to be ninety, her face would always have the trusting innocence of a little girl.

His heart grew big in his chest. How could

providence have been so generous to Jessie Ramming? First, to give him Anna; and now, after eight barren years, to give the two of them the promise of a child. It was perfect.

Too perfect. At the back of his mind, a warning sounded—a warning no louder than the dry whisper of a hidden rattlesnake. He resolved to stick closer to the house in the future, until the baby came. After today. After he had located the missing heifer.

To the west a half-day's ride across the rolling, infinite prairie, rode another man. Like Jessie he was tall and lean. But there the resemblance ended. This man rode in a slouch, his shoulders hunched high above the base of his neck, giving him the predatory look of a vulture. A tangle of black beard, streaked here and there with tobacco juice, concealed his face from his cheekbones to the grimy collar of his shirt. Below the shapeless gray hat only his eyes were visible. And they were not pleasant to look into, those eyes.

Beneath him, under a rundown saddle, was a raw-boned sorrel, ewe-necked and gaunt-ribbed, a horse with a treacherous temperament. They were a well-matched pair.

The sun stood squarely overhead when the bearded man caught his first sight of the two immense cottonwood trees that marked Jessie Ramming's place. He rode for another hour before he smelled the odor of burning mesquite roots and lye soap from Anna's washing. He spurred the sorrel mare into a thicket of mesquite trees, dismounted, and withdrew a rifle from the scabbard lashed beneath a stirrup leather.

Stooping low, until his long arms almost touched the ground, he moved carefully up the ridge that concealed the house from view. Near the crest of the rise he flattened himself against the ground and continued on, crawling awkwardly on elbows and knees. High above, in the azure blue of the cloudless sky, a brace of turkey buzzards circled silently, watching.

The man waited for a long time. A single bead of sweat slid down the bony ridge of his nose, hesitated an instant, then splattered against the scarred butt of the rifle. Finally he saw her come into view.

Excitement shot through him like a fever. Smiling Jack Sluder had never killed a woman before.

He reckoned it was two hundred yards down the slope to where she was hanging out clothes behind the little house. When he squeezed the trigger, she didn't pitch backward as he expected, but jerked forward against the shock of the heavy bullet. The faded blue shirt she had been reaching to hang on the line fluttered to the dirt.

From where he lay, Sluder couldn't tell where the bullet struck, but he saw blood and flesh and bits of bone mushroom from her back. He knew, as surely as the sun was blistering the back of his neck, that she was dead.

He watched without expression as she lay on her side in the alkali soil, her knees drawn up against her belly. Her mouth was opening and closing, but he was too far away to hear the words she was saying.

Without conscious thought, his left hand crept to the side of his head. The thin fingers played along a deep, ragged scar that began at the remnants of an ear and ran down into the tangled blackness of his beard. He turned his head and spat tobacco juice into the hard-caked earth, sending a horde of red ants into an aimless frenzy.

After a time, he backed away on his elbows and knees, cursing now and again in a ragged whisper as a knee or forearm impaled itself on a goathead thorn.

At last he rose stiffly, not bothering to dust his trousers, and walked with his stoop-shouldered gait down the slope to the sorrel. There he paused and looked for a long moment at the battered rifle in his hands. Then he shoved the weapon into the boot, mounted the restive mare, and rode westward, the way he had come. Behind him the woman still jerked occasionally in the dirt.

Jessie Ramming was whistling a song about a red-haired girl and a sailor when the shot sounded. The report came first to the ears of the gray gelding and he tossed his head, startling the heifer a few yards ahead.

The sound was the flat, angry slap of a rifle shot, not the thunder of a shotgun. Of that Jessie was certain. He drew the gelding to a halt, cocked his head to one side, and squinted his deep-set eyes.

The heifer saw her chance and lunged for the breastwork of mesquite trees lining the creek bed. Ramming didn't bother to glance after her. He was hoping that his ears were playing tricks. The only weapon he owned was his goose gun, fourteen pounds of eight-gauge thunder. The shot he had heard came from something else.

Abruptly he pulled his hat down tight and sent the gelding up the gulley at a dead run, toward the scant collection of buildings that comprised his home, a quarter-mile away.

But there was nothing to see, nothing out of the ordinary. Near the front door a wisp of steam rose from the heavy black wash pot that squatted in a bed of coals. The door itself was open, an invitation to any chance breeze on that warm autumn day.

"Anna!" he called, his deep voice unnaturally loud in the stillness of the afternoon.

In the corral a cow stopped licking the week-old calf at her side and lowed plaintively. It was the only answer to his call.

Quickly, and with growing urgency, he unsaddled the horse and strode toward the house. Ducking instinctively, he stepped through the doorway into the cool interior of the adobe. Only a meager shaft of light squeezed through the single tiny window and he squinted against the dimness.

"Anna?"

Fear was dammed behind the word.

He thought he heard a sound from somewhere in back. He moved through the single room that served as kitchen and sitting room into the bedroom, his boots booming hollowly on the rough planks of the floor. Returning to the kitchen he saw a covered pot on the stove and smelled the tanginess of stewing cottontail rabbit.

He was just outside the door when he heard the sound again. It was a weak sound, barely audible, and it made him think of a rabbit caught in a snare. The nerve endings along his spine grew cold and prickly. He stepped quickly to the corner, but all he could see was one end of the crude clothesline he had made for her.

An instant later he was at the rear corner of the house. When he saw her lying there his breathing stopped. His movements as he went to her seemed slow and measured, and everlasting.

She lay on her side, facing away from him. Her brown and white polka dot dress was powdered with gray from the alkali soil.

SEASON OF VENGEANCE

Where one shoulder blade had been there was now a large, ragged circle, stained a deep crimson.

Jessie knelt beside his wife and put one big, rough hand gently against the tumble of auburn hair lying along her temple.

"Anna! Anna!" he whispered.

Her eyelids fluttered weakly and she looked into his ashen face.

"I knew you'd come," she murmured. "I waited for you, Jessie."

As effortlessly as if she were a child, Ramming picked up the limp form. As he held her in his arms he saw that it was already growing late. The setting sun was staining the western horizon with rich shades of orange and purple. It was the time of day she loved best.

Walking slowly, almost on tiptoe, he carried her into the house and laid her on their bed. Blood, thickly dark, oozed onto the muslin sheet.

Ever so gently, he cut away the brown and white cloth from her chest. There, just were the swell of her left breast began, was the bullet hole. It wasn't a large hole, Jessie thought numbly. Only a small, black circle surrounded by waxen flesh that was already turning a cold shade of blue.

He turned her on her side and cried aloud. Where the soft lead projectile had exited was an angry mass of shattered flesh and fragmented bone. The mushrooming bullet had carried away a segment of her shoulder blade as broad as his hand, leaving nothing but a cavern of ragged membranes and shredded muscle tissue.

Like a man sleepwalking, Jessie gathered clean rags and liniment and began to cleanse the wound. He went outside to the big cottonwoods and stripped off quantities of bark for a poultice. Afterward, in the light of the coal oil lamp, he pulled a chair to the side of the bed and took her hand in his.

In the night she roused once. "If it's a boy, we'll call him little Jessie," she murmured softly.

Jessie went outside to the corral and cried.

Daylight brought a faint hope. Ramming freshened the bandage covering the great wound in her back. He bathed her forehead, talking to her in his deep voice, assuring her that all would be well.

Despite a sense of foreboding, he tore himself from the room. Behind the adobe house where she had fallen, he surveyed the slope for a time, then climbed the ridge to its crest. His search was brief. In minutes he had found the tell-tale sign.

Angrily, he wiped away a mist of tears and studied the unnatural furrow in the earth. The sign was elementary. There were the two indentations where the rifleman's elbows had rested when he sighted down the barrel of the gun, and two more gouged by the toes of his boots. A few inches to one side was the ragged pattern of brown where the man had discharged a mouthful of tobacco juice.

The rays of the morning sun touched an object all but hidden in the coarse blades of buffalo grass. As a man might handle a gem of inestimable value, Ramming picked it up carefully and deliberately. It was an empty brass shell casing, the scars of an imperfect breech girdling its lethal shoulder.

At last he stood and moved down the slope, away from the house. The faint succession of footprints led him to the cluster of mesquite bushes. There he spent another half-hour, painstakingly examining every scar in the soil, every track left by man and horse.

Finally, he followed the horse's tracks until there could be no question of its direction. Then he turned and hurried back up the slope, dread growing into a hard lump in his chest.

He found Anna weakened. The skin of her face was drawn and sallow. Her breathing was quick and labored. He cursed himself for having left her alone.

Time became an indistinct, shadowy tunnel. One instant the tiny window would be aflame with the noonday sun; the next it would be a black rectangle with nothing beyond. Sometime during the pre-dawn darkness of the fourth day, Jessie laid his head against his forearm at the kitchen table and slept. When he awoke and looked into her little girl's face, he realized that she looked old. There were dark circles about her eyes. Her mouth was a white line, drawn down at the corners.

He dropped to one knee beside the bed and took her face between his big hands. Her flesh was cold, like clay.

He held her hand in both of his until daylight. Then he went outside to dig her grave. He chose a spot among the towering cottonwoods and with a heavy-headed grubbing hoe attacked the earth like a man possessed. Three long years of swinging a pickaxe in a Trabajo gold mine had taught him that skill very well.

It was done quickly. He buried her deep, so

the coyotes and badgers couldn't reach her, and went back to the house.

He strode purposefully to the bedroom and, reaching up, removed the shotgun from the pegs that held it above the door. Seating himself on the edge of the bed, he drew the gun from its oiled sheath and held it out before him.

It was a massive weapon, a breech-loading eight-gauge of French manufacture. The dual, thirty-six-inch barrels could reach out and bring down a goose flying as high as the clouds. Or so his Grandfather Asa had said when he bestowed the gun on Jessie's father. And no one argued with Captain Asa Ramming, not even after the anchor chain of his packet ship snatched off his leg and fed it to a hungry mako shark through the hawsehole.

But Jessie's father never fired that shotgun. Francis Ramming was a bookish man, a schoolteacher, to the everlasting disappointment of Captain Asa. And when Francis made a gift of it to his son Jessie he did so contritely, as he would an object of the devil's own design.

The shells were in a corner of the steamer trunk. Jessie opened the box to fill his pockets and saw that not a cartridge was missing. He had never quite gotten around to shooting Captain Asa's goose gun. Now, testing its weight in his hands, he felt an eerie chill, the sensation that comes with inevitable peril.

Outside, at the corral, he dropped the bars of the gate and watched the cow and calf trot away to freedom. Coyotes would have that little one before the sun rose tomorrow.

The gray horse whinnied as he approached, and pushed its head against his chest. Ramming shoved the muzzle aside roughly and set about saddling. When he spoke, his voice had a tone that made the gelding shift uneasily.

SEASON OF VENGEANCE

"The world's not big enough to hide that man, gray."

For the span of a deep breath, Ramming rested his head against the gray horse's neck, then he swung into the saddle and rode toward the ridge behind the house. At its crest he pulled up and turned in the saddle. It looks exactly as it always has, he thought. Except for the fresh mound of earth there beneath the cottonwoods.

It will not be quick.
It will not be easy.
But Jesse Ramming will get his revenge.

Read the complete Bantam Book available, April 1st, wherever paperbacks are sold.

MEET THE DERBY MAN—
THE NEW WESTERN POWERHOUSE

Look sharp, hit hard—
that's the Derby Man's style.
He's a fast-moving mountain of muscle
who throws himself into the thick of
the West's greatest adventures.

14185-6   THE PONY EXPRESS WAR
by Gary McCarthy $1.75

The Pony Express—a grueling 2,000 mile race through hell. The pace and terrain are deadly enough but vengeful Paiute warriors and murdering saboteurs led by a sadistic giant threaten to turn the route into a trail of blood. Until one man has the brains and brawn and guts to save the Pony Express—The Derby Man.

14477-4   SILVER SHOT
by Gary McCarthy $1.75

It's hard-rock mining and rock-hard brawling as the Derby Man takes on a boom town. A man could mine fabulous wealth on the Comstock but the Derby Man strikes only a motherlode of trouble. With his sledgehammer fists and sharply honed wits he sets out to expose a spellbinding stock manipulator.

**These Derby Man adventures are available
wherever Bantam Books are sold.**

Watch for the next Derby Man adventure

EXPLOSION AT DONNER PASS

It's the Derby Man to the rescue when the Central Pacific Railroad challenges the towering Sierras and a mysterious wave of terrorism threatens every hard-won foot of track. The workers' tempers are seething, the winter snows are mounting and suddenly, trapped like the members of that ill-fated wagon train years before, Darby must conquer Donner Pass or die.

A Bantam Book available June 1st wherever paperbacks are sold.

"REACH FOR THE SKY!"

and you still won't find more excitement or more thrills than you get in Bantam's slam-bang, action-packed westerns! Here's a roundup of fast-reading stories by some of America's greatest western writers:

☐ 14207	**WARRIOR'S PATH** Louis L'Amour	$1.95
☐ 13651	**THE STRONG SHALL LIVE** Louis L'Amour	$1.95
☐ 13781	**THE IRON MARSHAL** Louis L'Amour	$1.95
☐ 14196	**SACKETT** Louis L'Amour	$1.95
☐ 14183	**PAPER SHERIFF** Luke Short	$1.75
☐ 13679	**CORONER CREEK** Luke Short	$1.75
☐ 14185	**PONY EXPRESS WAR** Gary McCarthy	$1.75
☐ 14475	**SHANE** Jack Schaefer	$1.95
☐ 14179	**GUNSMOKE GRAZE** Peter Dawson	$1.75
☐ 14178	**THE CROSSING** Clay Fisher	$1.75
☐ 13696	**LAST STAND AT SABER RIVER** Elmore Leonard	$1.75
☐ 14236	**BEAR PAW HORSES** Henry	$1.75
☐ 12383	**"NEVADA"** Zane Grey	$1.95
☐ 14180	**FORT STARVATION** Frank Gruber	$1.75

Buy them at your local bookstore or use this handy coupon for ordering:

Bantam Books, Inc., Dept. BOW, 414 East Golf Road, Des Plaines, Ill. 60016

Please send me the books I have checked above. I am enclosing $_____ (please add $1.00 to cover postage and handling). Send check or money order —no cash or C.O.D.'s please.

Mr/Mrs/Miss_____

Address_____

City_____ State/Zip_____

BOW—3/81

Please allow four to six weeks for delivery. This offer expires 9/81.

LOUIS L'AMOUR 1

BANTAM'S #1
ALL-TIME BESTSELLING AUTHOR
AMERICA'S FAVORITE WESTERN WRITER

- ☐ 14931 THE STRONG SHALL LIVE $2.25
- ☐ 14977 BENDIGO SHAFTER $2.50
- ☐ 13881 THE KEY-LOCK MAN $1.95
- ☐ 13719 RADIGAN $1.95
- ☐ 13609 WAR PARTY $1.95
- ☐ 13882 KIOWA TRAIL $1.95
- ☐ 13683 THE BURNING HILLS $1.95
- ☐ 14762 SHALAKO $2.25
- ☐ 14881 KILRONE $2.25
- ☐ 20139 THE RIDER OF LOST CREEK $2.25
- ☐ 13798 CALLAGHEN $1.95
- ☐ 14114 THE QUICK AND THE DEAD $1.95
- ☐ 14219 OVER ON THE DRY SIDE $1.95
- ☐ 13722 DOWN THE LONG HILLS $1.95
- ☐ 14316 WESTWARD THE TIDE $1.95
- ☐ 14227 KID RODELO $1.95
- ☐ 14104 BROKEN GUN $1.95
- ☐ 13898 WHERE THE LONG GRASS BLOWS $1.95
- ☐ 14411 HOW THE WEST WAS WON $1.95

Buy them at your local bookstore or use this handy coupon for ordering:

Bantam Books, Inc., Dept. LL2, 414 East Golf Road, Des Plaines, Ill. 60016

Please send me the books I have checked above. I am enclosing $_____ (please add $1.00 to cover postage and handling). Send check or money order —no cash or C.O.D.'s please.

Mr/Mrs/Miss_____

Address_____

City_____ State/Zip_____

LL2—4/81

Please allow four to six weeks for delivery. This offer expires 9/81.

LUKE SHORT
BEST-SELLING WESTERN WRITER

Luke Short's name on a book guarantees fast-action stories and colorful characters which mean slam-bang reading as in these Bantam editions:

☐	13679	CORONER CREEK	$1.75
☐	13585	DONOVAN'S GUN	$1.75
☐	12380	SILVER ROCK	$1.50
☐	14176	FEUD AT SINGLE SHOT	$1.75
☐	14181	PAPER SHERIFF	$1.75
☐	13834	RIDE THE MAN DOWN	$1.75
☐	13760	DESERT CROSSING	$1.75
☐	12634	VENGEANCE VALLEY	$1.50
☐	14183	WAR ON THE CIMARRON	$1.75
☐	12385	THE SOME-DAY COUNTRY	$1.50

Buy them at your local bookstore or use this handy coupon for ordering:

Bantam Books, Inc., Dept. LS, 414 East Golf Road, Des Plaines, Ill. 60016

Please send me the books I have checked above. I am enclosing $_____
(please add $1.00 to cover postage and handling). Send check or money order
—no cash or C.O.D.'s please.

Mr/Mrs/Miss_____

Address_____

City_____ State/Zip_____

LS—2/81

Please allow four to six weeks for delivery. This offer expires 8/81.

Bantam Book Catalog

Here's your up-to-the-minute listing of over 1,400 titles by your favorite authors.

This illustrated, large format catalog gives a description of each title. For your convenience, it is divided into categories in fiction and non-fiction—gothics, science fiction, westerns, mysteries, cookbooks, mysticism and occult, biographies, history, family living, health, psychology, art.

So don't delay—take advantage of this special opportunity to increase your reading pleasure.

Just send us your name and address and 50¢ (to help defray postage and handling costs).

BANTAM BOOKS, INC.
Dept. FC, 414 East Golf Road, Des Plaines, Ill. 60016

Mr./Mrs./Miss_____
(please print)

Address_____

City_____ State_____ Zip_____

Do you know someone who enjoys books? Just give us their names and addresses and we'll send them a catalog too!

Mr./Mrs./Miss_____
Address_____
City_____ State_____ Zip_____

Mr./Mrs./Miss_____
Address_____
City_____ State_____ Zip_____

FC—9/75